THE PHANTOM CORRAL

THE PHANTOM CORRAL

Bliss Lomax

GUNSMOKE

First published in the UK by Wells Gardner

This hardback edition 2009
by BBC Audiobooks Ltd
by arrangement with
Golden West Literary Agency

ISBN 978 1 405 68288 6

British Library Cataloguing in Publication Data available.

Printed and bound in Great Britain by
CPI Antony Rowe, Chippenham and Eastbourne

CHAPTER 1

"YOU'VE GOT TIME TO SPARE," Zack Trilling, the Bar 7 foreman, said, glancing at his watch as he sat at breakfast with Rainbow and Grumpy. "Hallett will get you into town thirty to forty minutes before your train is due. Chances are Number 3 will be late; she usually is."

"We've got to stop at the bank for some money," Grumpy declared. "We better be movin'."

He pushed back his chair and started to get up.

"Keep your rompers on a minute," Rainbow told him. "I've got to have another cup of coffee. You've been straining at the bit ever since I wired Conroy we'd take the case."

"I want to git it over with," his pint-size partner returned, with his usual crustiness. "It don't sound important to me. It's jest goin' to bust up our plans for a long lazy summer, here on the ranch; that's about all."

Trilling smiled at their bickering. It struck a very familiar note in his ears, and he was reminded once again that the success they had achieved in their profession had changed them very little. Rainbow Ripley and Grumpy Gibbs were famous today. Though they still referred to themselves simply as range or stock detectives, they had long since outgrown the limitations of that phase of detective work and won renown in a dozen Western states in the general field of criminal investigation.

But Zack, who had grown old as the efficient foreman of Judge Carver's Bar 7 outfit, liked best to remember them as they were when they were riding for the brand: Rainbow, a tall, soft-spoken young man, and Grumpy, a doughty, hard-headed fighting bantam, already turned fifty, even in those days.

"How long do you boys expect to be gone?" he asked, as Rip filled his cup.

The tall man shrugged.

"I don't know, Zack; maybe Grump is right about it and it won't amount to anything. We've worked for the Conroy and McCann Construction Company before. They were building that big Fox Lake power dam at the time, and someone seemed to be interested in slowing up the work. We handled that easily. This seems to be about the same proposition."

"Railroad this trip," Grumpy put in. "Rocky Mountain Short Line job. Branch line up to Eureka. They can't git the men to stay with the work, labor turn-over every few days. It's slowin' things down, of course."

"Nothing very startling about that," said Zack. "You boys ought to be able to get to the bottom of it without putting any strain on your talents."

"That's my idea," the little man grumbled. "We'll be lucky to git a week's work out of it." He scowled at Rip. "Is it goin' to take you all mornin' to finish that coffee?"

The crew had finished breakfast and most of the men were waiting to see the partners off.

"Here come your passengers," Snuffy Willis called to Hallett as Rip and the little one stepped out with Zack. "Don't make a mistake and deliver them dudes to the wrong address. The way they're rigged out yuh might think they was a couple of bank presidents if yuh didn't know 'em."

"Shucks, a fella couldn't go wrong that-a-way, once the little runt opened his mouth," old Arizona, the dean of the Bar 7 riders, cackled.

Rainbow joined in the laughter; he knew he and Grumpy had no better friends anywhere. The little one came back with a bristling retort, however.

"A brayin' jackass always sounds loudest in the mornin'. This suit I'm wearin' is new, but if you had half the polish I've got on the seat of these pants, you might have walked off with that cross-eyed woman in the railroad eatin' house."

The cross-eyed woman was a tender point with Arizona, and the laugh was turned on him at once.

"Git out of them overalls once in a while and educate yorself a little, Arizona," Grumpy called back with a chuckle as Howie set the team in motion. "Nice bunch of boys," he remarked to Rip and Howie. "I always hate to leave 'em."

Rainbow nodded. They had been coming back to the Bar 7 between cases for many years and had come to consider it home. Proof that the ties that bound them to this Black Forks country were to endure was to be found in the fact that for a long time they had been acquiring range north of the ranch and stocking it with cattle, which Bar 7 worked under an arrangement they had made with the judge.

"I wish I was goin' down to Denver with you fellas," Howie remarked, as he touched up the team. "If I had your money, I wouldn't be spendin' my spare time in the wilds of Wyomin'."

"What's the matter with Wyomin'?" Grumpy inquired.

"Nuthin' particular. But I ain't been no further away from the ranch than Green River in two years; and that don't get a man nowheres. They used to have a good rodeo over there, but we're puttin' on a better show right here in Black Forks of late."

A smile flowed into Rainbow's gray eyes.

"When you've been around a lot, you begin to realize there's considerable about Black Forks that'll stand up with the best you can find anywhere." He jerked his head in the direction of a distant ranchhouse. "I've noticed that it isn't only fast horses that old Pike Kendrick raises."

Howie grinned.

"If you mean Resa Kendrick, you're sayin' somethin'. But Stark Tremaine's got her all fenced in; no one else has got a chance with her. And no hard feelin's about it," he added generously. "Stark's a nice guy."

"He's all of that," Rainbow agreed. "Grump and I are going to need a foreman one of these days; we can't impose on the judge forever. If he won't let us have a Bar 7 man for the job, I hope we'll be lucky enough to get Stark."

Hallett shook his head.

"Not much chance of that," he declared. "Harley Purcell will never let him get away from Double Diamond. When old Norcross finally has to call it a day, Stark will step into his shoes. He's just as good as ramroddin' that big spread right now. . . . Hi, you Bess, Baldy!" he shouted at the team. "Shake your legs! We got a train to catch!"

They were in town with time to spare. After a brief stop at the bank, Howie drove them to the station. Rip went in for the tickets. When he came out, he found Grumpy and Hallett standing up in the buckboard, their attention focused on a cloud of dust that was moving down the flats to the east of town.

"We're going to have some time to kill," said Rainbow. "Number 3 is running forty minutes late at Granger. . . . What's all the excitement?"

"Reckon it's Mustang Smith and his bunch bringin' in some broomtails," Hallett answered. "I know they been out on the desert for a month or so. . . . Yep, that's what it is! Got a snag of 'em this time."

The bands of wild horses that roamed the far reaches of the Red Desert had been so thinned out during the past few years that sight of the big *caballada* being driven into the railroad shipping pens was something of a novelty in Black Forks.

Mustang Smith's outfit had been luckier than usual this trip and they had almost two hundred head in the bunch they were hazing across the flats this morning.

The horses seemed to realize that this was their last run, and they were making it a wild one. Eyes gleaming, wild as eagles, they whirled repeatedly and tried to break back to open country. Always, Mustang Smith and his men were ahead of them and turned them in time. But sight of town and the railroad that was soon to carry them off to Salt Lake City, to be ground up into chicken feed, filled the wild things with a last, desperate resolve to break free. With manes flattened and tails flying in the wind, they dashed down the bottom lands along Black Forks Creek, whipped its placid waters to spray in crossing, and flashed out toward the road north.

This maneuver had been tried before, and Smith and his men were ready for it. A ranch fence ran at right angles to the road. All the mustangers had to do was to close the open gap to the east.

"By grab, they'd have made it but for Sam Pedroli's fence!" Grumpy exclaimed disappointedly. "I was kinda pullin' for 'em. They know they're licked now. Comin' in without any fight left in 'em."

The shrill cries of the mustangers and the screaming of the frightened horses had not gone unnoticed in town. Young and old headed for the shipping pens for a look at the broomtails.

But they were not the only ones whose interest had been captured by sight of the wild ones. Up the creek a few hundred yards from the town bridge that crossed the stream at the U. P. station, was a cabin, made of discarded railroad ties, the shack was half hidden in the willows that grew tall and green along the stream. Standing in the doorway, anger and resentment whipping through his under-nourished body, Johnnie Smiley had been watching the horse herd almost from the moment it had appeared on the flats.

Johnnie was a boy of fifteen, spindly shanked and with a crop of yellow hair that always needed cutting. He had a pair of blue eyes to go with his yellow hair, and a fine, sensitive face that was stamped already with the hard knocks of life.

Things had never been easy for Johnnie. His faded overalls and butternut shirt were shabby with long wear and well patched, but they were clean, and he was scrupulously clean himself.

"They're gittin' 'em into the pens," he said over his shoulder to his father, who sat in the darkened room, weaving a willow basket. The boy's tone was bitter. "They wasn't harmin' no one, out on the desert. Gittin' so men will do anythin' to make a dollar."

Being only a kid—in fact he was often called the Kid, and when that was not definite enough, the Black Forks Kid—Johnnie knew about those big beef herds which once had come bawling down from the north in the flush days, when Texas cattle were being fattened in Wyoming and range was free, only from hearsay. His own memory ran back only to lean pickings for his father and himself, to more and more barbed wire and fewer and fewer jobs. What the end was to be, he didn't know. But sight of these luckless broomtails going to their ignominious end came close to giving him the answer. He knew Mustang Pete Smith, Bill Ambers and the rest of that outfit. In their way, they were all right; they were only trying to make a living, and he tried not to hold it against them. But he was asking too much of himself; he was too fond of horses for that, and the fate that awaited these broomtails aroused his pity. It bit deep into him because in his subconscious mind he saw a parallel between them and himself; he knew what it meant to be pushed around, not wanted.

He turned away from the door, his young face sober with his thinking. From a tin can that stood on a shelf in back of the stove, he took fifteen cents, pausing for a moment to estimate how much money remained in the can. He shook his head over it, for he was the real breadwinner of the family and had to regard himself as a man.

"When the ponies are gone there won't be much of anythin' wild left in this country," he muttered grimly. "Reckon that's the way some folks want it. The way things are goin', they might as well divide everythin' between a few big outfits and be done with it."

"No use takin' on that-a-way, son," Mr. Smiley answered without looking up from his weaving. He had the basket almost finished. He held it up and turned it around in his hands. "This is a extry specially nice one, Johnnie. It ought to bring a dollar, at least."

He was a mild-tempered little man with the innocent unwrinkled face of a child, and slowly going blind with cataracts. The top of his head was bald and had taken on a fine polish. Around his ears, little tufts stood out like balls of cotton. In happier days, Wash Smiley had been Black Forks' leading saddle-maker.

"Wild hosses ain't wuth nuthin'," he observed without interest. "They're all runty with inbreedin', and hoofs so soft from drinkin' alkali water that you can't git a shoe to stay on 'em."

"Mebbe they ain't worth nothin', Pappy," the Kid admitted reluctantly, "but it ain't right to grind 'em up into chicken feed."

Mr. Smiley nodded. "Seems a shame," he agreed. "Used to be lots of wild hosses around when I fust come to Black Forks. Onct in a while you could trap a good one. Made a fair to middlin' cow pony. That was before yore time, Johnnie."

The boy clamped on his battered hat.

"Purty bright out," he said. "You stay inside today and keep out of the light, Pappy. Yore eyes botherin' you much this mornin'?"

" 'Bout as usual."

"You need an operation," the Kid said soberly. "I hope I can git you down to Salt Lake City this winter."

"Whar you goin' now?" his father inquired. "I need tobacco."

"I know; I got the fifteen cents. Reckon I'll drop over to the shippin' pens before I come back. I want to have a look at the horses."

He struck off down the path along the creek and climbed to the road at the bridge. His long, free-swinging stride carried him into town quickly. His lean, narrow-hipped figure was a familiar one in Black Forks. Buck Rainsford, the sheriff, gave him a friendly greeting as he passed.

"Mawnin', Kid," Buck drawled. "I figured you'd be down to the railroad by now, lookin' over that wild bunch."

"Goin' down directly, Buck," the Kid answered. "Had to git some tobacco for Pappy." He started on again, only to turn back after taking a step or two. "By the way, Buck, you ain't heard of no one lookin' for a man, have you?"

The sheriff found no reason to smile.

"No," he said. "Things are awful quiet. But somethin'

will be turnin' up; there's others waitin' and hopin' too."
He jerked his head to indicate the three cowpunchers
roosting on the wooden steps in front of the Mint Saloon.
"Cowboys without horses," he muttered more to himself
than to the boy. "Too bad! . . . Well, fall's comin' and
things will pick up about rodeo time. I'll let you know if
I hear of anything, Kid."

Rainsford was on his way to the courthouse. He crossed
the street, his grizzled face a little rockier than usual, for
under his walrus hide, he was a kindly man.

"Fifteen—and an old man already," he murmured,
thinking of Johnnie. He shook his head over it. "Seems
like a boy ought to get a better break than that."

Down at the railroad station, with time to spare, Rainbow and Grumpy had crossed the tracks to the siding and
climbed up on the plank catwalk that ran around the top
of the shipping pens. Mustang Pete Smith spied them and
came around to where they stood watching the milling
horses. A cloud of dust was rising from the pens, but the
brisk west wind whipped it away as soon as it rose.

"Pete, you rounded up quite a bunch of 'em this time,"
Howie greeted him. "You wasn't out more than two
months."

"Jes about. We did all right. At eight dollars a head, it
runs up to sixteen hundred dollars, more or less. I see you
and the little fella are all slicked up, Rip. You off ag'in?"

"A little business in Denver," Rainbow answered. "How
far out were you, Pete?"

"That broken country around Sioux Rocks. Awful dry
this year; no water at all standin' in the *charcos*. I figgered
they'd have to come into the springs at Sioux Rocks." He
was referring to the horses and he indicated them with a
jerk of his head, spattering one with an accurately aimed
stream of tobacco juice at the same time. "I guessed
right for onct."

The broomtails were long in hair and shedding in spots.
It gave them a ragged appearance. Most of them were
smaller than the average cow pony, and inbreeding had

had the curious effect of making their heads seem too large for their bodies.

The partners and Howie moved around the pens with Mustang Smith. It was precarious going, for a score of men were perched on the catwalk and the only way to pass them was to step around them. Leading the way, Rip had reached the last pen and was turning back on the side nearest the main tracks, when he ran into the Kid, who had been there some minutes, his attention focused on a fiery buckskin stallion that stood a good four hands higher than any other horse in the pens.

"Hi ya, Rip—Grumpy!" Johnnie exclaimed, as they stopped.

"What are you doing in town?" Rainbow inquired. "I thought you were out at Double Diamond."

"No, I asked for my time last week. You won't catch me workin' for that outfit no more."

"What went wrong?" Rip asked.

"I had a run-in with Mundy. That big wolf dog of his bit me a couple times and I said I wouldn't feed him no more. Mundy slapped me around; he wouldn't pick on nobody his size."

"Wal, what about old Pike?" Grumpy demanded. "You always seemed to git along fine with him."

"He said he'd have to string along with his foreman. That settled it."

The conversation suddenly interested Howie Hallett. He poked his head over Grumpy's shoulder.

"There's something wrong about your story, Kid," he said. "Pike Kendrick told me only last week that you was goin' to ride Black Lightnin' for him again at the rodeo."

"Did he?" the boy grunted, his mouth tight. "Wal, he's foolin' himself. If he's going to race any horses, he'll have to git somebody else to do his ridin'—as much as I need the money."

"You needn't worry about finding a mount," Rainbow told him. "You can get more out of a horse than any boy around here; Pedroli or one of the Bushfields will be glad to have you."

The Kid's starved boyhood had always touched Rip in a soft spot and Grumpy and he had often put the lad in the way of earning a few dollars.

"I noticed that big buckskin had taken your eye, Johnnie," he continued. "Good long barrel on him. Nice chest, too."

"He looks all right," the boy agreed. "Got as clean a pair of forelegs as you'd ever want to see. A four-year-old, I reckon. No broomtail about him. Look at him now!"

The big buckskin was fighting mad. Squealing with rage, it reared up and tried to leap the high fence. Failing in that, it swung around and attacked the pen with its hind legs, trying to kick it down.

Mustang Smith yelled at one of his men, who came running with a coiled rope and drove the buckskin back, cursing it to a finish before he was through.

"That yaller devil is the orniest critter I ever laid eyes on!" Mustang growled, wiping his perspiring face on his sleeve. "Raised hell ever since we trapped him!"

The big horse stood out in the pen, trembling, lips rolling away from its teeth.

"Good blood in him," Grumpy observed thoughtfully. "He musta busted away from some ranch when he was a colt."

"There ain't no mark on him," Mustang spoke defensively at once. "He was runnin' wild when we trapped him. Reckon that makes him ourn."

There was a heavy-footed humor of a sort in Mustang Smith. Thinking to have a little sport at Johnnie's expense, he said:

"If you could break that buckskin, Kid, you'd have a hoss that'd knock the spots off Pike Kendrick's geldin'. Yes, sir! You could make yorself some real jack."

"I don't know whether he can run or not," the boy replied.

"You can buy him cheap—eight bucks," Mustang offered solemnly. It was cruel in a way; he knew the Kid didn't have half of eight dollars to spend on a horse of any kind. "I'd give you a bill of sale that would shore enough make him yourn. That prize money counts up five hundred dollars. It would sit you right up in business."

He was laying it on rather thick, but Johnnie was too taken with the prospect to be suspicious. But not Rainbow. Grumpy saw the tall man's face harden with displeasure.

"I'd shore like to own him," the Kid declared. "Reckon I could gentle him; I kind o' got a way with horses."

The mustanger laughed at his own jest.

"I was jest kiddin'," he said, with a grin. "I wouldn't sell that hell-cat to you, Kid. He's an outlaw; he'll kill you if you ever tried to toss a saddle on him."

"I wouldn't care about him bein' an outlaw," said Johnnie, disappointment pinching his face. "It's the eight dollars that sticks me."

"Wait a minute," Rip spoke up. He glanced at Mustang. "You had your little laugh, Pete, but you made a deal. The buckskin belongs to the Kid. You come into the depot with me and write out that bill of sale; I'll give you the money."

"Rip—you mean it?" the boy burst out excitedly.

"Sure, I mean it. You'll need something for feed too. Here's a twenty-dollar bill. You can pay it back some time."

"I shore will!" the boy declared earnestly.

Rip and Grumpy were fifty miles east of Black Forks an hour later. Their talk went back to the boy.

"It was foolish of you to buy that horse for him," the little one declared heatedly. "You won't feel so good about it if that outlaw bangs him up. Old Wash Smiley depends on the boy to earn the livin'."

"Johnnie won't get banged up," Rainbow returned lightly. "They'll get along all right together."

"Good Josephine, you don't expect that buckskin to amount to anything, do you?"

"No, but the way that boy's face lit up was worth ten times twenty dollars to me. He'll pour out all the love that's in him on that horse. That's all I was thinking of, plus the fact that I don't like to see a man make game of a defenseless kid. . . . We better drop off a wire to Conroy at Rawlins, telling him we'll be in Denver tomorrow noon."

CHAPTER 2

WHEN THE PARTNERS WALKED into the Conroy and Mc-Cann offices, thirteen months had passed since they were there last. Rip sent their names into Conroy.

"Some changes around here," Grumpy observed. "That blonde secretary seems to be gone."

"Married, I suppose," Rainbow said idly. "She was too good-looking to last long in a big office."

Without waiting, the blonde secretary's successor showed them into Conroy's private office. The latter greeted them heartily.

"I'm sure glad to see you gentlemen," he said. "I hope you can get to the bottom of this trouble as quickly as you did on that Fox Lake job. I presume my letters have given you some idea of what we're up against."

"Only in a general way," Rip replied. "We want you to go into detail about it. I suppose you've got a deadline to meet on the contract."

"Naturally! We thought we allowed ourselves all the time we'd need, but the way things are going it'll take us forever to build that ninety miles of track. We've got about two hundred men on the job. We can't get any work out of them. I don't mean the track-layers and our field crew; it's the pick and shovel gang. Fifty to sixty a week ask for their time. We send a new bunch up and the same thing happens all over. It's enough to knock hell out of any job."

"Who is supplying you with men?"

"Sam Strait, the labor contractor. We've done business with Sam for years."

"He's tricky, accordin' to what I hear," said Grumpy.

Conroy nodded. "I suspected Sam had something to do with this right away. I went into it thoroughly and didn't get anywhere. Anything to interest Sam Strait has to have a profit in it. I couldn't figure out how he could make an extra dollar by double-crossing us. After all, we're one of his biggest accounts. He collects a lot of money in labor fees through us."

"It's an old game for these labor bosses to put men on one job, collect the fee, then pull them off and ship them on to another job and collect a second time," said Rainbow.

"That's not the case this trip," Conroy answered with a trace of irritation. "The answer isn't going to come as easily as that, Ripley. It's the men who pay the fee; they're not so dumb as to pay their two dollars and stay with us a week, lose three or four days getting to another contractor and then have to shell out a second time. No, sir! It's going to cost us a thousand dollars for every day we run over our deadline. McCann is East. I've talked to him long distance a dozen times. He's got the idea some competitor of ours is trying to get our scalp. I don't agree with that."

"What do you think?" Rainbow asked.

"I don't know what to think. The Rocky Mountain Short Line got five bids on this job. I know the other bidders. They're all responsible firms and good friends of ours. There's plenty of work around; they're all busy. Thinking one of them might have the knife out for us doesn't make sense to me."

They discussed the matter for some minutes.

"You payin' the standard wage?" Grumpy inquired.

"We're paying a dollar and a quarter; that's better than the scale. The grub's good. We always keep a clean, comfortable camp. . . . Now you fellows tell me what the answer is."

"We'll have a try at it," Rip told him. "Is there anyone up there who'll recognize us?"

"Mike Moran, our construction boss, will remember you. There'll be a train up this evening. I'll give you a letter to Mike."

"We won't go up to the job right away, Mr. Conroy. I

believe we'll get further if we find out what we can in Denver, first. We'll put up at some cheap hotel and get into some old clothes and hang around the saloons and pool rooms down Sixteenth Street near the station and see what we can hear. We'll brace Strait for a job later on. You write Moran that he isn't to recognize us when we show up; and you do the same if you run into us. We won't be sailing under our own names, of course."

"All right," Conroy agreed. "I want you to have a free hand. But get us some results, Ripley. You know what we'll be up against in that high country if we're not done before snow flies."

He walked to the door with them twenty minutes later.

"Will I be hearing from you?" he asked.

"We'd better stay away from here," the little one advised. "There's a good chance that yore offices are bein' watched."

Rainbow found the suggestion a plausible one.

"If we have any word for you, we'll get a message through," he said.

The elevator carried them down to the street.

"What do you make of it?" Grumpy asked.

"I don't know; but Sam Strait's got a finger in it; it couldn't be otherwise."

"By grab, we're agreed on somethin' for once; let's go over to the Eidelweiss and have a good lunch before we start slummin'. It'll perhaps be the last good meal we'll be meetin' for some time."

After lunch, they stepped into a cheap clothing store, carrying their bags. They made some purchases and changed clothes in the store. When they came out they were dressed in the rough garb of day laborers.

"These leather bags are a give-away," Rip remarked. "We'll check them at the depot this evening and buy a couple cheap suit-cases. Where's the hotel you mentioned?"

"Around the corner on Sixteenth Street. Argos, they call it. It's a dump."

They found the Argos and registered under assumed names. For the rest of the afternoon, they circulated

among the beer saloons and pool rooms within a block of
the Union Depot. Though Grumpy was a past master at
scraping acquaintance with strangers they picked up nothing of interest until about five o'clock, when they saw a
score of men coming across from the depot. They had
the look of construction job laborers. A burly red-headed
individual seemed to have them in tow.

"That bunch has just come in off some job and is headin'
for the nearest drinkin' establishment," Grumpy observed.
"They're totin' their suitcases and bundles—that's a purty
good sign they've got through somewheres."

The men passed within a few feet of the partners. The
red-headed one, who seemed to be in charge of the gang,
said in a voice that could have been heard half a block
away, "You buckos have got only time to hoist a couple
beers; your train pulls out in twenty-five minutes."

They hurried into the saloon on the corner.

"Let's tag along," Rainbow suggested. "See if you can
strike up some conversation with them, Grump. Maybe we
can find out where they're from and where they're going."

The partners managed to crowd up to the bar. Grumpy
picked out his man and purposely stumbled over the latter's roll. He bent down and straightened it up against the
bar.

"Didn't see yore roll settin' there," he told the owner.
"Guess there was no harm done."

"None at all," the man answered. "We all flocked in
here together; got only a few minutes in Denver."

"I see you all look like yo're travelin'. Where you
headin'?"

The man glanced down the bar at the red-headed man
and lowered his voice in answering. "Nevada. Guffey is
keeping it kinda quiet."

Grumpy spun a silver dollar on the bar and invited the
man to have a drink with them. The stranger was not ad-
verse to accepting the proffered hospitality.

"Nevada's a long piece away from here," the little one
remarked. "Big job out there?"

"Yeh, Western Pacific is buildin' to the Coast. Good

pay, too. A dollar and a half a day, and our time starts when we pull out of Denver. . . . Here's looking at you!"

Grumpy set down his empty glass.

"A dollar and four bits a day sounds good to me and my pardner. They ain't payin' that kind of money in Colorado. I reckon a buck a day and eats for swingin' a pick is about what we can expect. We just hit town; been workin' up in Montana."

"You can do a little better than that," he was told. "There's a job up on the Rocky Mountain Short Line. Paying a dollar and a quarter. We was up there about a week when this comes along. Nice money, and we're gitting paid for three or four days without doing a lick."

"Is there any chance of the two of us horning in?" Rip inquired.

Guffey, the red-haired man, came shouldering up to them.

"What's all the gabbing about?" he demanded angrily of the man who had been supplying the partners with the information they wanted. "I told you to keep your mouth shut, Davis."

"It's just a couple of guys looking for a job, Guffey," Davis protested. "They'd like to go out with us."

"Would they?"

Guffey scrutinized the partners suspiciously. And then, apparently satisfied that they were what they pretended to be, he said, "If it's a job you're looking for, drop around to see Strait in the morning." He pulled out a business card bearing the labor contractor's name and office address. "Tell Sam I sent you in; he'll fix you up with something. Can't arrange any transportation for you this evening."

Guffey turned away, and Davis tipped the partners a wink.

"That guy blows off purty loud," he told them. "But he don't mean nothing. You see Strait; he'll treat you right. If he offers to send you up to Eureka on that Short Line job, take him up; you won't be there long. Sam will have you headed for Nevada in a couple weeks or less."

Rainbow put on a puzzled look.

"That sounds all right, but I don't get it. If Strait is shipping men out to that Western country right along, what's the idea of sending a man up to this other job for a couple weeks?"

"I dunno," Davis replied. "Guess he's got to wait till he gets an order for men before he can fill it. But you don't have to worry about that Short Line job; I didn't raise a sweat the whole time I was up there. You can take it easy 'cept when Moran, the company super, is around. . . . You sure you won't have another drink?"

"We got to run along," Grumpy told him. "I got to pick up a pair of boots I left to be repaired."

The partners left the saloon and started looking for a reasonably clean restaurant in which to have supper.

"We shore hit the jack-pot that time," Grumpy declared, with a chuckle. "This thing is just about what I figgered it was. If some contractor out in Nevada is offerin' more money and a bonus of three or four days' pay, he's going to git men."

"But why the attempted secrecy? Why send men to one job only to pull them off in a week or so?" Rip shook his head. "We're a long way from understanding Strait's game."

They surprised themselves by finding a good Mexican restaurant. After supper, they spent the evening as they had the afternoon but without learning anything that shed any further light on what was wrong with the Conroy and McCann job at Eureka.

A few minutes after nine next morning, they walked into Sam Strait's shabby office. Others were there ahead of them and they had to wait their turn.

A partition divided the office. Every few minutes Strait came to the door and called someone in. He had the hard, rocky face of a man out of whom the last drop of softness had been wrung. He finally motioned for the partners to step into his office.

Grumpy told him Guffey had sent them around. Strait jotted down their names.

"I can send you to Eureka this afternoon at a dollar and a quarter a day," he growled. "That okay?"

"If it's the best you got," the little one told him.

"It's all I've got for the present. Something better may come along. You'll find Ed Ferguson up here. He'll keep in touch with you. Here's your transportation. Be at the depot at four o'clock. You'll find Guffey there. There'll be some others going up."

He signified that he was busy and hurried them out.

Back on the street, Rip said, "That was short and to the point. Looks like we're going to raise a crop of blisters for a few days."

"Takin' this case was yore idea, don't forget it!"

The tall man laughed. "It still seems to be a good idea," he said lightly.

They crossed the street to a poolroom and killed an hour watching Strait's place. All they saw was the usual ebb and flow of life around an employment office. Men came and went; others stopped to read the Help Wanted ads neatly chalked on the blackboard that hung outside the windows.

"We've had enough of this," said Rip. "Let's get out."

They had just reached the door when an argument started across the street. Guffey stood barring the way to a man, not much bigger than Grumpy, who was determined to get into the office.

"I tell you to go 'long and peddle your papers, Joe," Guffey insisted with what he considered great patience. "Sam ain't got no time to waste on you. If you got a raw deal out there it ain't Sam's fault."

"The hell it ain't!" the man retorted angrily. "He knew he was handing us the works when he shipped us out. We all got the same dose. The rest can stand for it if they want; but not me! I paid my own fare back to Denver for the satisfaction of busting Sam Strait in the nose, and I ain't changing my mind now!"

He lowered his head and tried to dive into the office. Guffey caught him under the jaw with a long, whistling right that lifted him off his feet. The man picked himself up and came back swinging with both arms. His courage and determination fell far short of being a match for Guffey's huge fists, and the latter proceeded to give him a merciless beating that had Grumpy wincing before it was over. Rainbow sensed what was running through his partner's mind.

"Hold your shirt on," he warned. "I'd like to take a hand in this, myself, but we can't afford to mix with Guffey and Strait just now."

A policeman appeared. He seemed to be well acquainted with the red-haired Guffey. "What's the trouble, Pat?"

"Just a bindle stiff who figures he's got a grudge against Sam," Guffey explained. "I tried to talk him out of it, but he wouldn't have it that way."

The policeman nodded and pulled the man on the sidewalk to his feet. "Git goin' now," he advised, "or I'm callin' the wagon!"

He gave the man a shove, and the latter stumbled away.

"Things can't be so good out in Nevada," Rainbow remarked, as he and Grumpy turned down the street. "I imagine it's that dollar and fifty cents a day."

"Most likely," the little one growled. "These rats git a man out there, where there's no other jobs around, and it's a buck a day for him, and he can like it or lump it. That's treatin' men like cattle. Helpless men, too."

Rip looked down at him thoughtfully. "Sounds like you're working yourself up about this."

"I am!" the little man snapped. "I'm shore gitting interested in Mr. Sam Strait—blisters and all!" He glanced across at the man with the battered, bloodied face. "We takin' a chance on bracin' that gent?"

"He might save us a long trip out to Nevada," Rainbow declared. "We'll tag along and see where he goes."

The man turned the corner, and halfway down the block, entered a cheap lodging house.

Moving with the aimless gait of men who are only killing time, Rip and Grumpy approached the door. They found no one in the downstairs office, and without stopping they ascended the stairs. An old man in shirtsleeves, obviously the clerk of the establishment, confronted them.

"What you boys want?"

"We just saw Joe come in," Grumpy told him. "We want to see what we can do for him. He looks purty tough."

"Hunh!" the old man grunted. "Looks like a train hit him! Who worked him over that way?"

"We dunno. What room is he in?"

"Nineteen, down the hall."

The old man clumped down the stairs, and the partners went on to room nineteen. Rip knocked on the closed door. Getting no answer, he pushed it open and walked in, with Grumpy at his heels. They found a gun leveled at them.

"If Strait sent you lugs around to finish me off, I'm ready for you!" they were told.

"Put down your gun," Rainbow said. "Sam Strait's no friend of ours. We're working for Conroy and McCann."

"Detectives?"

"Yeh. If you want to square your score with Sam Strait, you'll talk fast. We overheard what you said to Guffey. What's your name?"

"Joe Pickens. . . . What do you want to know?"

"We want you to tell us what you ran into out in Nevada. You were promised a dollar and a half a day by Strait. Did you get it?"

"For the first week, then it was a buck a day, take it or leave it. Guys that Strait sent out before us told us what the game was, but we wouldn't believe it. They knew what they was talking about."

"You were to get a bonus for the time lost in getting out there. Was that paid?"

"Guffey handed it to us before we left Denver. Each of us got a five-spot."

The partners found the circumstance peculiar enough to make them prick up their ears.

"Wal, that clears things up somewhat!" Grumpy declared weightily. "A construction company working as far away as Nevada wouldn't hand out bonus money in that way; they'd wait till the men was on the job and add it on to the first pay envelope. Strait's handin' out that money for someone else."

"Was there any talk about it, Pickens?" Rainbow asked.

"Naw, suckers don't think! We stuck the money in our pants and figured we was being treated real square. It didn't get to us that Strait was using us for saps to put Conroy and McCann in the hole. When I hit Denver, I shoulda gone right up to the Eureka job and did my talking there; that would've stopped the double crossing crook!"

"We'll do something about it," said Rip. "You can't stay here, Pickens; Strait will have you picked up and bundled out of Denver. Are you broke?"

"Just about."

Rainbow gave him twenty-five dollars.

"That'll keep you going for a few days. We'll hide you out for a week or so. I want you to keep off the streets and be sure not to do any talking. Can you get out of this place into the alley?"

"Yeh, there's a back stairs."

"All right," Rip told him. "We'll get a rig; you meet us in the alley in ten minutes."

After Grumpy had peered out into the hall and found the way clear, Rip and he hurried down to the street.

"We better hire a hack; that'll be quickest," the little one advised. "Plenty of 'em in front of the depot."

"We'll grab one in a hurry," Rainbow answered. "We don't want to waste any time about putting this man Pickens under cover."

They climbed into a hack and had the driver make a quick turn around the block and up the alley. It hadn't taken them more than seven or eight minutes at most. There was no sign of Pickens. But they had told him to be down in ten minutes.

The seconds ticked away, however, and still he failed to appear.

"We're kiddin' ourselves, Rip," Grumpy growled. "We

been waitin' five minutes already. They got to him, shore as shootin'!"

"I'm going up to the room," Rainbow rapped. "You wait here."

He ran up the back stairs and disappeared inside. The door of room nineteen stood open. There was no one there. Pickens' canvas roll was gone, too. An overturned chair suggested that there had been a struggle.

Rip returned to the hack and told the man on the box to drive on.

"Gone, eh?" Grumpy snapped.

"Yeh, bag and baggage. They must have grabbed him a minute or two after we left. We could have used Pickens."

"No use lookin' for him now." The little one shook his head disgustedly. "We're just out twenty-five dollars."

"I'm afraid we're out more than that." Rainbow's gray eyes narrowed grimly. "The way this thing was timed makes it look as though we'd been spotted. If Strait's put the finger on us, we've got a rough time staring us in the face on the Eureka job; and we'll not get very much for our trouble."

"Good Josephine, if you feel like that about it, why bother with goin'? If we ain't foolin' nobody—"

"That's the rub, Grump! We don't know whether we're fooling Strait or not. The only way we can be sure where we stand is to go through with our play and take that train this afternoon."

CHAPTER 3

THERE WAS GOOD GRASS on the flats along Black Forks Creek. Johnnie put his big buckskin on it, safely picketed. Possession of the animal had changed his world completely, and for the first day or two he spent most of his time seated on the cabin doorstep, watching every move the horse made.

The stallion was as wild as Mustang Smith had said it was. The Kid was not discouraged when he saw it stand stiff-legged for hours at a time, head raised and eyes rolling; he knew it was fear and that it would gradually wear off. When the big horse began to pick at the grass, he was overjoyed.

"He's comin' around all right," the Kid told his father. "Grazin' a little this mornin'. What he needs right now is to be left alone."

"Wal, if he can't be broke, he may turn out to be a good bucker and you can sell him to Burrell when he brings his wild string up to the rodeo. A bucker usually brings a good price."

Johnnie squared his thin shoulders indignantly.

"No, sir, Pappy; I'll never sell that fella! Reckon I'll have chances aplenty one of these days," he added confidently. "But he's my horse; nobody's goin' to git him away from me."

It was seldom that anyone was to be seen along that stretch of the creek, save for the town boys, who came down to fish for bullheads. Though they were of his age, Johnnie had little in common with them and, hungry as he was for companionship, had never encouraged them to stop at the cabin. He was glad of it now; it meant that he had the horse to himself and didn't have to worry about anyone trying to go near the animal.

The money Rainbow had given him had not been put in the coffee can that held the dwindling family nest egg; the money was for the horse, and the Kid intended to keep it separate. He had not often had as much as twenty dollars at one time. To guard against it being lost or stolen, he had placed it in a tobacco bag and wore it around his neck on a string. It was with a distinct feeling of importance that he walked into the bank one morning and had the bill changed. He proceeded to Rinehart's general store, then, and purchased a bag of oats, which he trundled home on his wheelbarrow. His father heard him coming. Wash wagged his head disapprovingly over spending money for grain.

"Seein' how little we got fer ourselves, seems like it's jest squanderin' money, buying grain fer a hoss."

"Pappy, that's what Rip said it was for. It wouldn't be right to use it for anything else." The boy pulled out a bag of candy from his pocket. "Mose took off ten cents 'cause he didn't have to deliver. I bought you some of them lemon drops." He handed his father the bag. "You always like to suck on 'em."

The old man took the bag and popped one of the yellow balls into his mouth and sucked on it noisily for a moment or two. He wasn't altogether mollified.

"The hoss ain't going to work out fer us, Johnnie. A job will be turnin' up fer you sooner or later and you'll be goin' out to one of the ranches ag'in. That'll leave me here alone. Don't seem as though I could look after a hoss, least of all a wild critter."

"Mebbe a job will turn up right here in town. Town jobs are more steady than ranch work. If I can git somethin' like that it'll be fine; I can look after you a lot better, and I could take care of the horse, too. By the way, Mose says he needs some more baskets. He sold that last one right off. He paid you a dollar and a quarter for it, Pappy."

Johnnie's spirits had bounced back with the thought of finding a job in town. It seemed to be the answer to all his problems. He gave his father the money he had received for the basket. The extra quarter, as well as Mose Rinehart's approval of his handiwork, pleased Mr. Smiley.

"I knew that was an extra nice one," he declared proudly. "If my eyes was what they should be, I could turn out four to five a week like that. . . . Hand me the can, Johnnie. I always like to drop the money in myself. Kinda makes me feel good. Whyn't you catch us a mess of bullheads fer supper? They're about the best eatin' there is, this time of the year."

"I'll git a good mess as soon as the sun gits off the water," the Kid promised. "I'm goin' to start cuttin' some willows this afternoon; I can make a brush corral that'll hold the big fella. If I have to go out on the range to work, havin' the horse in a corral will make it easy for you;

you can throw him a little feed in the evenin'. Before the
cold weather comes, I'll knock a stable together. There's
lots of good boards left out at Rinehart's old icehouse.
I asked Mose about it; he said I could help myself. We'll
be all right if I can just keep some money comin' in."

Building a brush corral was not something that could be
started and finished in one afternoon by man or boy working single-handed. The Kid worked methodically, and as
the days passed, he began to have something to show for
his labor. The big buckskin had become accustomed to
seeing him move about. He had begun to graze contentedly
and no longer bounded away to the end of his picket rope
every time he caught sight of the boy. When fresh water
was poured into his tub, he'd come in for it as soon as
Johnnie withdrew. After he had drank his fill he would
stand there swishing his dripping muzzle in the water.

The Kid had placed a wooden box alongside the tub. In
it he began to leave a few handfuls of oats. The big horse
found them and devoured them greedily.

Johnnie came to the cabin door several mornings later
to find the horse with its head in the empty oat-box. The
buckskin looked up and nickered at him. The boy's heart
overflowed with happiness.

"Gosh, you know me!" he exclaimed, his throat tight
with emotion. The temptation to try to put his hand on
the buckskin's glistening muzzle almost overcame him, but
he resisted it. "It's too soon for that," he told himself. "He's
beginnin' to figger things out in his own way; one of these
days he'll understand he ain't got nothin' to be afraid of."

Mr. Smiley finished another basket that he pronounced
the equal of the one Mose Rinehart had sold so quickly.
Johnnie took it into town. When that errand was finished,
he sauntered up the street. He knew the cowboys lounging
in front of the saloons. He stopped to speak to half a dozen
or more, inquiring half-heartedly about a job. They shook
their heads and expressed the opinion that it would be
another month before the big outfits began to take on
extra men for the fall work.

"I gotta git somethin' before then," he thought, as he

moved on. "Must be somebody in Black Forks could use me."

He was in some doubt as how best to proceed. The *Gazette* ran a column of want ads. He considered that means. It would cost forty cents. Before he spent the money, he decided to ask Buck Rainsford what he thought about it.

The sheriff's office was around the corner in back of the courthouse. The Kid went there and spoke to the sheriff.

"I don't want to do Carl Spitzer down at the *Gazette* out of forty cents," the sheriff declared, with a chuckle. "But I don't think it's going to be necessary for you to do any advertisin'. You hurry yourself around to Dan Messenger's office. He's up there right now. We were speakin' about you last evenin'."

The Kid's face lit up.

"You mean he's got a job for me, Buck?"

"You talk that over with him," Rainsford replied. "He'll be in court this afternoon; you catch him before he goes home to dinner."

Since Judge Carver had been elected to the bench, Dan Messenger was universally recognized as the county's leading attorney. His offices were located on the second floor of the two-story corner building he had recently erected on the town's main street. The bank and a doctor and dentist occupied the lower floor; upstairs, in the rear, were some small unfurnished apartments.

Messenger was at his desk, in an inner office, dictating some letters to his stenographer, when Johnnie walked into the waiting-room. The connecting door stood ajar, and the lawyer called to him to sit down.

The Kid knew Dan Messenger in the same way he knew everyone in Black Forks. This was the first time, however, that he had been in his office. The walls were lined with shelves of law books. Along with the steel engravings of Washington and Lincoln and framed facsimile of the Constitution, they had a sobering effect on the boy. It seemed incredible to him that a man could know all that was stored away in these bulky volumes. Somehow, it made him acutely aware of his own lack of what was commonly referred to as "book learning." He had often heard the story of how Dan Messenger, a penniless cowpuncher, had come in off the range and read law in Anson Carver's office for four years, supporting himself by doing chores and odd jobs. It had never made much of an impression on Johnnie till now. In a way, he found a spark of inspiration in it.

"Reckon if you want somethin' bad enough, you can git it," he mused. "It don't mean you have to be smart enough to be a lawyer."

"Come in, Johnnie!" Messenger called. "Close the door and we won't hear the machine; Mrs. Lamb has some typing to do. How is your father?"

"He don't have much to say about it, but his eyes are gittin' worse all the time, Mr. Messenger. As soon as I can git my hands on the money, I'm goin' take him down to the city. Doc Treadway told me some time ago that it was too late for medicine to do any good. He says an eye surgeon can remove the cataracts."

The lawyer nodded sympathetically, and though Treadway, whose office was downstairs, had told him it was equally too late for an operation, he said, "If Doc feels that way about it, you haven't any reason to give up hope. . . . Johnnie, I know you like ranch life. I can understand that; I used to like it myself. Still do, in fact. What I'm getting around to is where I can induce you to work for me. I need someone to look after the building and keep it neat. I've just lost the man I had."

"I'd like it fine," the boy declared without hesitation. "I talked it over with the old man a few days ago, and I told him the best thing for me to do was to find somethin' in Black Forks. That way, I could look after him better; and there's another reason now, Mr. Messenger; I've got a horse that needs attention."

Messenger leaned back in his chair and laughed merrily. He was a thin, wiry man, his hair now shot with gray. His lean face had never lost its range tan.

"Buck was telling me Rainbow had staked you to a

horse. I can imagine you want to stay close to him. Buck says he's wild as a bat. You haven't had a saddle on him yet, have you?"

"No, sir! I haven't even had a hand on him. If yo're goin' to git anywhere with a horse, you've got to have patience."

"That's not a bad thing to have whatever you're doing. Does he look like he can run, Johnnie?"

The Kid grinned. "I'm shore hopin' he can, sir. Looks to me like he's built for it. He's a big fella, Mr. Messenger; not a mark or blemish on him."

The lawyer smiled at the boy's enthusiasm.

"Sounds to me like you've got an idea buzzing in your head. When you're ready to invite me, I'd like to come down and have a look at him. But to get back to this job, Johnnie; the hall and stairs will have to be swept down every morning, as well as the sidewalk. You can use a hose on the walk once or twice a week. There's a washroom that has to be kept clean. In here, the waste baskets have to be emptied and things dusted. Mrs. Lamb can tell you exactly what to do. Just don't disturb any papers. If you get down early, you'll be through by nine o'clock. You can go up to the house then and help Mrs. Messenger for an hour or two. That will leave you free for the rest of the day. I'll pay you twenty-five dollars a month. Treadway and the dentist will be glad to pay you something for looking after their offices. Does it sound all right to you?"

"It sounds wonderful," the Kid said, a little overwhelmed by his good fortune. "That's big money for me, especially if the job is steady."

"It will be steady," Dan assured him, happy that he could afford to be generous with the Kid. His own boyhood years had been lean ones, too. In fact, he could see himself all over again in many ways in Johnnie Smiley. "I'd like to have you begin tomorrow morning. Seven o'clock will be early enough. The folks in the apartments don't like to be disturbed before then."

The boy told him he'd be there on the dot, and Dan took him out to Mrs. Lamb. She gave him a key to the building and showed him where the brooms and other things were kept. When he reached the street, the Kid was walking on air. He hurried back to the sheriff's office with his good news.

"I can thank you for all this, Buck. You'll never be sorry you recommended me to Messenger."

"I'm sure I won't, Kid," Rainsford said in his lazy drawl. "But, pshaw! I didn't have to urge Dan to take you on; he's had his eye on you for some time."

"Yeh?" the boy queried, a little surprised. Buck nodded.

"You've got some friends, Kid."

Within a few days the boy's life had fallen into a definite pattern. He was accustomed to being up and about by five. His first concern was to care for his horse. He cooked breakfast, then, and left for town. He was always back by early afternoon; it left him free to spend long hours with the big buckskin. He had never been so happy. One evening he inched along the picket rope and put his hand on the animal's muzzle. The big horse trembled under his touch but did not bolt. It was the beginning of a strange surrender.

"Gosh, you'll be a beauty when you'll let me put a brush and curry comb on you," he glowed. "I'll have something to show Rainbow when he gits back."

Dan Messenger often mentioned the horse to him.

"I'm still waiting to be invited down to see him, Johnnie," he reminded the Kid as they met on the stairs. He noticed that the boy had outfitted himself with a pair of new overalls. That he had pride in himself did not surprise Dan.

"I want to wait till I've had a saddle on him once or twice," the Kid told him. "It won't be long now, Mr. Messenger; he let me brush him down last evenin'. I'm going to turn him into the corral this afternoon and see how he likes that."

"Have you got a saddle?" Dan asked.

"I got an old stock saddle. It's purty heavy but it'll do."

Dan nodded and started to continue up to his office. He stopped after taking a few steps.

"Johnnie, when you go up to the house, you tell the wife I said to let you have the saddle I've got hanging in the basement. I never get a chance to use it anymore. If you like it, you can have it. Your father will remember it; he made it for me."

"Gosh, I couldn't take it for nothin', Mr. Messenger," the Kid protested. "I'd shore like to have it if you'll let me work it out."

Dan pretended to be annoyed.

"What's the matter?" he demanded. "Rainbow can give you a horse, but I can't give you a saddle. Don't I rate with Rip?"

"It ain't that," the boy answered apologetically. "I'm workin' now; I figger I ought to pay my way."

"All right," Dan relented. "You try it out. We can make some arrangement later."

"Whar did you git that?" Mr. Smiley demanded, when Johnnie walked into the cabin at noon with the saddle slung over his shoulder.

"Take a good look at it, Pappy," the boy told him, lowering the saddle to his father's knees. "Does that fancy toolin' on the skirts look familiar to you?"

Mr. Smiley stared and stared and ran a trembling hand over the beautifully embossed leather rosettes. Emotion overcame him for a moment.

"Eight years old, and still as tight as a drum," he said with faltering voice. "I made 'em right and they stayed right if they wa'n't abused."

"Do you remember who you made this one for, Pappy?"

"Shore! Dan Messenger. He used it to go huntin' up in the Solomon Mountains. Is he loanin' it to you, Johnnie?"

"No, he said I was to try it out and if I liked it, he'd make a dicker with me."

Old Wash looked up, aggrieved.

"There ain't no question about yore likin' it, is there?"

"No, Pappy; it's one of the last saddles you made, and I'm ready to work my fingers off to keep it. I'll be needin' it one of these evenin's."

The need came sooner than he expected. The buckskin grew used to the corral. It wasn't long after that before Johnnie was leading him around with a hackamore.

The hackamore gave way to a bridle. It was a trying experience for both horse and boy. The miracle was that it succeeded. Dan shook his head when the Kid told him what he had accomplished.

"I know you're telling the truth, Johnnie, but if you went down the street right now you wouldn't find one man in fifty who'd believe it could be done. If that horse will stand for the feel of the bit, he'll take a saddle."

The Kid hung his new saddle on the corral gate for a day that the buckskin might accustom himself to sight and smell of it. Dropping it on him proved less difficult than getting him to take the bit. Until dark, the boy walked him up and down the flats, gradually tightening the cinch strap but making no attempt to mount. But that moment wasn't far away now. After supper the next evening, he led the horse across the creek to the dirt road that ran out to Rinehart's abandoned icehouse. They had the road to themselves. The boy knew it was now or never; that when he swung up he had to stay with the stallion or begin all over again, with the likelihood of never succeeding.

The Kid got a foot up and vaulted lightly into the leather. The big horse froze in its tracks for a moment. The unfamiliar weight on its back filled it with terror. Suddenly it left the ground and tried to trade ends in mid-air. The Kid kept up a stream of talk, but it seemed to be wasted on the horse. It reared up on its hind legs and tried to shake him off. Failing in that, it lowered its head and plunged off into the sage to do some desperate sun-fishing. The Kid stayed with him and finally straightened him out. The stallion began to run. Johnnie swung into the road. It was better than a mile out to the icehouse. The boy's blood began to sing as he felt the play of muscles beneath him and saw the long, clean legs flashing out like pistons. The horse was in a lather when Johnnie pulled him up.

"Man, you can travel!" the Kid burst out exultantly. "Yore soft, and you ain't shod, but I can take care of that! When you've been brought into condition there won't be a cold-blooded horse around here that can stay with you!"

He ran his hands over the long muzzle and fondled the animal's ears as he let him get his breath.

"We'll take it easy goin' back. Yo're a purty fancy crow-hopper, big fella, but you ain't no shucks as a bucker; you ain't mean enough for that."

When they got back to the flats, he walked the horse until he had him cooled out. In the early dark, he rubbed him down carefully, talking to him as he worked. As Rainbow had predicted, he had something on which to pour out his love at last, something of which he could be proud. His arm stole around the buckskin's arched neck.

"I gotta have a name for you, mister," he whispered. "Yo're goin' to be a champion. . . . Gosh! That's what I'll call you—Champ! I couldn't ever find a better name!"

CHAPTER 4

DESPITE ALL THE DIFFICULTIES they were having, Conroy and McCann had pushed construction of the Rocky Mountain Short Line's new branch as far as the little mining town of Aurora. Steel had been laid several miles beyond the town; the roadbed was half completed for another three miles. The construction company had moved its camp to the new railhead only several days before Rainbow and Grumpy arrived from Denver with eighteen other men who had been shipped up to the job by Sam Strait.

The partners found the little tent city spread out along the banks of a rushing creek that supplied it with crystal clear mountain water. With the flaps of the walled tent, which they shared with four other men, rolled back, they had a million dollar view of the Divide and the Medicine Bow Range. Being new, the camp was clean. As for the grub, it was plain, but there was plenty of it and the work they were doing gave them an appetite to appreciate it. However, as the end of the week neared, the conviction grew on them that they were wasting their time.

"You had it right," Grumpy muttered, as he and Rainbow sat on the bank by themselves just before dark. "They spotted us in Denver. Strait tipped Ferguson off pronto. That's the only way I can explain why he hasn't opened up to us."

Rip skittered a stone across the stream.

"No question about it," he said thoughtfully. "I don't know whether Strait knows who we are, but he's certainly got it figured out that we're working for the company. It makes me wonder why he hasn't tried to have us roughed up. It wouldn't have surprised me if we'd been jumped in the Denver depot or thrown off the train in the yards."

"They don't know how much we know, Rip," the little one asserted. "That's why Strait is bein' cagey with us. Otherwise, he'd have had us slugged before we hit camp."

Rip shook his head dubiously.

"I don't know whether that's the answer or not. It seems to me this game is so thin that if we know anything it's a case of knowing too much for Sam Strait's racket. Maybe we've been too cautious. Most of the gang will be going into Aurora tomorrow night to tank up. Suppose we trail in, too; if they've got anything up their sleeve, we'll give them a chance to come at us. There's no point in breaking our backs this way if it isn't getting us anywhere."

"You're right," Grumpy growled. "Moran caught me with my boot off this afternoon and hobblin' around with a cramp. I thought he was goin' to bust out laughin' before he looked the other way and got past me."

Obviously, Strait had not been suspicious of them when they were in his office, else he would hardly have identified Ed Ferguson as his undercover agent on the Eureka job.

That had come later, when they had followed Joe Pickens to his room. Just how it had happened had ceased to interest the partners. But Ferguson, a colorless man with a heavy, rather stupid-looking face, continued to claim their attention. He had been on the job from the first, and Mike Moran, the company superintendent, had rewarded this seeming loyalty by making him sub foreman. It had given Ferguson a chance to move around and talk with the men, which was exactly what he wanted. He had stopped that soon after Rip and Grumpy hit camp. He was so careful not to have anything to say to anyone that he might as well have said in so many words that he knew he was being watched.

"You don't expect all the men who go into Aurora tomorrow night to come back, do you?" Grumpy asked. "They'll have their week's pay in their pocket."

"We'll lose a bunch of them," said Rip. "Ferguson isn't the only man Strait's got working for him; he hasn't been passing any word around but that doesn't mean it hasn't gone out. We're losing at least one man in our tent."

"Who, Rip?"

"Petersen. He had his roll spread out when I walked in on him. I asked him what he was doing. He said he was just looking for a needle. He was packing up. . . . We better turn in; we're both tired."

Moran could have ordered a work train run into Aurora on Saturday evening to carry the men in for their fling. He had discovered by experience, however, that that was only making it easier for many of them to desert. Without a train to take them in, the only way to reach town was to hoof it. The long walk seemed to deter no one who was of a mind to go. Some didn't even wait for supper. By seven o'clock, half the camp was moving in the direction of Aurora.

Rip and the little one trudged along with a hundred others. The temporary release from work, coupled with the prospect of pleasure immediately ahead, brought out a rough, noisy good-fellowship. It was not extended to the partners. Even their own tent-mates had drawn away from them.

"You'd think we had the ten-year itch and it was catchin'," Grumpy commented sourly.

"I suppose Strait has had it spread around that we're professional labor spies," Rainbow said. "I didn't see anyone toting his roll when we left camp. But look up ahead now; I can count a dozen or more. Someone brought the stuff out and cached it along the right-of-way during the day. . . . There goes another man down the embankment. It's Petersen."

It was only minutes before Petersen climbed back to the tracks. His bindle was slung over his shoulder.

"Nice goin'!" Grumpy jerked out with a characteristic grunt. "At this rate, Moran's goin' to lose forty to fifty men this week. I don't know as it's any skin off our teeth; we were hired to find out how this racket was bein' worked and who was behind it, not to stop it; that's up to Conroy."

Rainbow agreed that was the case.

"We haven't done so badly, Grump. Before the night's over we may be able to put our finger on the four or five men—there can't be more than that—who are working with Ferguson. We can pass that information along to Conroy and he can weed 'em out. That'll put it up to us to find out who's behind Strait. He may be picking up a few dollars by shipping men out to Nevada, but it's not the real pay-off. Someone's handing it out to him in big chunks."

The Short Line was already running two stub trains a day into Aurora. One left in the morning and the other in the late afternoon. The men who were leaving the job were satisfied to spend the night there, carousing with the others. The town had only two saloons. By eight o'clock it was almost impossible to pack another man into them. This happened to be Saturday night for Aurora's hardrock miners as well, and they were a tough-minded gentry who didn't take kindly to being pushed aside by a rag-tag construction gang. Arguments broke out almost immediately.

"Looks like this town may come apart at the seams tonight," Grumpy observed, as he and Rip took a turn up and down the main street.

"Things will be popping in another hour," Rainbow predicted. "That's the depot ahead of us. We'll wander down there later on; if a play's going to be made to grab us, that'll be a good place for it; it's dark there."

They turned back, their carelessness nicely feigned. They knew what they were inviting; that if they were downed it would be some time before they saw Aurora and the camp again. Grumpy was prepared for action; he had a gun concealed in his shirt.

Several cautious storekeepers were putting up the wooden shutters over their windows. The partners were passing a darkened shop, when a low whistle reached them from the shadows. They glanced that way and saw a man standing in the doorway, his hat pulled low over his face.

"I saw you fellas pass a few minutes ago," he said guardedly. "I been waiting for you to come back. There's a church just around the corner. Walk up that way; I'll follow you."

"Who are you?" Rip demanded.

"It's Joe Pickens. You ought to remember me. We had a little talk in Denver."

The partners saw now that this was the man who had disappeared from the rooming house.

"Okay," Rainbow told him. "We'll meet you in front of the church."

He and Grumpy were frankly surprised to find Pickens in Aurora.

"He's asking for another beating, showing up here," Rainbow observed.

"Mebbe not," was Grumpy's suspicious rejoinder. "This could be a come-on for us; that gent could have changed bases since we saw him last and be playin' it Strait's way."

Ripley agreed that that was possible.

"We'll be set for whatever comes up," he said. "If this bird happens to be on the level, we can turn a trick to-night that'll tie a knot in somebody's tail."

They reached the church. They had been there only a few seconds when Pickens joined them.

"I didn't run out on you with your dough," he hastened to tell Rip. "You'd only been gone a couple of minutes when I heard somebody at the door. I thought it was you fellas. Guffey and a big punk I used to see around Strait's office comes barging in. Before I can grab my gun, the big guy whams me on the head with a billy. They must've dragged me into the alley and got me down to the freight yard, 'cause I'm on my way to Ft. Worth in a box car when I come to. A railroad dick finds me. They stick me in a hospital in Amarillo for a couple of days. Money, gun, even my four-bit stickpin gone. They didn't leave nothin'. I rode the rods back to Denver and borrowed dough enough to get me up here."

It sounded like the truth to Rip.

"What are you going to do now?" he inquired.

"I'm going to bust the thing wide open!" Pickens burst out angrily. "After what I been handed, I'm getting even with Sam Strait if it kills me! I didn't pull in until this morning. I was going out to the camp. Then I figured it was Saturday and the gang would be in tonight and that this was the place for me to tell the suckers what they're falling for. But I don't want to queer anything for you; I took your money, so I guess it's up to me to listen to what you've got to say about it."

"What you're suggesting would be all right if you could get the men to listen to you," Rip said, after thinking it over for a moment. "You know Strait's got some of his gang planted up here. If—"

Grumpy muttered a warning, "Hold it Rip! There's a couple men walkin' this way. This could be it."

The two men who had turned the corner sauntered past the church and looked them over. Though it was dark on the tree-lined street, the partners had no difficulty recognizing the men. They had seen them on the job, day after day.

"Who are those crumbs chasing—you fellas or me?" Pickens asked bluntly.

"Maybe all three of us," Rainbow answered. "Do you know them?"

"The shorter of the two is Bill Doxey. I always figured he was a stooly gent. I didn't get the other one."

"He calls himself Torchy Wright," Grumpy told him. He was satisfied that Pickens was not trying any double-cross. "What do you know about Ed Ferguson?"

"The rat!" Pickens growled. "He's working for Strait. It was Ferguson who rigged things up for me and the bunch that went out to Nevada together. He and Doxey were thick. That's what tipped me off to Bill."

"Who else was close to Ferguson?" Rip inquired.

"No one that I remember. I suppose Strait's moved in some more guys since I left. That was some weeks ago, now. But what's the idea of those guys tailing you? Has Strait got your number?"

Rainbow grinned.

"That seems to be the situation. We came into Aurora tonight to give his boys a chance to jump us. We figured if they did that we'd have our answer and also learn who Ferguson has working with him. You say you want to blow things wide open. If that means you don't mind sticking your neck out, with a fair chance that the roof may fall in on all three of us, we'll try to tear into them with you."

Pickens nodded grimly. "All you've got to do is say the word."

"All right," Rainbow agreed. "We know Ferguson is in the saloon next door to the hardware store. Most of the crowd is in there, too. Let's see if that's where the pair that just passed is heading. If we can get them all together, we can make this count."

They retraced their way to Aurora's main street and were in time to see Doxey and Wright elbow their way into the saloon.

"The next thing to do is to see if there's a back entrance to the place," Ripley told Grumpy and Pickens.

They hurried around the block and found an unfenced lot in back of the saloon. Empty beer kegs and a miscellaneous collection of bottles and boxes left little doubt that the building could be entered from the rear.

"Here's a door," Grumpy announced. He tried it and found it unlocked. He pushed it back and walked in. He was gone a few moments.

"How does it look?" Rainbow asked.

"Just a storeroom between us and the bar. The inside door won't give us any trouble; I tried it. If it's yore idea for us to waltz into this dump, there ain't nothin' to stop us."

"Just getting in won't be enough," the tall man remarked soberly. "There's been a lot of liquor going down the hatch in there; it's not going to be easy to get the attention of that mob and make them listen to anything, to say nothing about what Ferguson and his friends will do about it. If we give them a chance to yell spies and labor baiters at us, we'll be licked before we get started."

Grumpy growled, "By grab, we've stuck up tougher crowds than this and made 'em say uncle! I guarantee you if I git in there and clumb on top of the bar and show 'em the business end of a gun I'll git some attention!"

After mulling it over for a moment or two Rainbow said in his quiet way, "All right; we'll play it along that line. You and Joe stick here and give me a couple minutes to get around in front. I'll fire a rock through a window; that'll draw attention and cause commotion enough for you to reach the bar. When you hear the glass break, rush in, climb up on the bar and slap a shot into the ceiling to show them you mean business. I don't have to tell you how to handle that part of it. When you've got them herded back against the wall, I'll walk in. You keep out of sight, Joe, till I call you. Have you got that?"

"Sure! But what do we do if something goes wrong?"

Rip glanced at him sharply.

"What's the matter, are you getting shaky?"

"No," Pickens whipped back.

"Then don't worry about what we'll do if something goes wrong; if this thing explodes in our face, we'll be stuck with it."

CHAPTER 5

IN BLACK FORKS, THE BRIDGER HOUSE was the only hotel worthy of the name. It was patronized chiefly by stockmen and their families and the traveling salesmen who worked the territory. There was a bar in connection where anyone looking for a game of poker could be accommodated. Grat Collamore ran the games. Being a professional gambler had not lowered his standing in the community. It fact, Grat was generally regarded as an upright citizen. He was a corpulent man, invariably coatless, addicted to fancy suspenders and sleeve garters, and a far cry from the sleek, debonair gambler usually encountered in the story papers. He had a favorite chair on the veranda of the Bridger House, and he could be found there every afternoon, armed with a palm leaf fan and a cigar.

It was a point of vantage from which he could watch the life of the town, in which he appeared to find an endless interest. He was seated there when Joe Mundy, the tall, black-haired Arrowhead foreman, passed. He nodded to him, and Mundy stopped.

"Did you come in alone, Joe?" he inquired.

"No, Miss Kendrick came in with me. She had some shopping to do. Have you seen the Smiley kid around?"

"Yes, he seems to be doing the chores at Messenger's place. I was surprised to hear Pike had let the boy get away from him. I took it for granted he'd have the Kid riding Black Lightning again this year."

"It was my fault," Mundy volunteered. "He rubbed me the wrong way and I lost my temper. The old man wants me to patch things up with him and get him back. It's up to me to eat crow. I'm glad to do it as long as Pike feels as he does; he's convinced the Kid can get more out of the horse than some other boy."

"I believe he's right about it," Collamore said frankly. "Naturally, I'm interested; there'll be a lot of money bet on the race this year. With the Kid up, Black Lightning is sure to repeat. I hope you don't have any trouble making Johnnie see it your way."

A smile touched Mundy's wide mouth. The bone structure of his face was pronounced, the cheek bones high and the skin tight over the bridge of his nose. It gave his countenance a rather dour but strong and not unhandsome appearance.

"That'll be easy," he said with the complete confidence which characterized any opinion he offered, whatever the subject. He was often wrong, but he found ways of making it seem otherwise. It made him appear to have more drive than he really possessed, though since Pike Kendrick had brought him down from the Windy River country and put him in charge of his big Arrowhead spread, Mundy had proved himself a capable, hard-working foreman whose loyalty to the brand could not be questioned. "He won't stick with a mop and broom very long when I start talking horse to him, Grat. That kid's got to have a horse around him or he isn't happy."

Collamore slapped at an offending insect with his fan.

"Your reasoning is all right, Joe, but it may not get you very far. The Kid happens to have a horse. Ripley and his partner were in town a couple of weeks ago when Mustang Smith and his crew drove in with a big bunch of broomtails. Rip bought one of them for Johnnie. I hear he's got it in a corral down on the flats."

Mundy laughed. "That's one on me; I thought for a minute you were going to tell me Pedroli or Ira Bushfield had signed him up to ride one of their horses. The Kid's got no business playing with a wild horse; he doesn't know anything about breaking a bronc."

"Maybe not." Collamore was silently amused. "For not knowing anything about it he's done pretty well. He's riding that animal. Charlie Ebbetts, the station agent, told me he saw him the other evening; the Kid was running the horse out on that dirt road to the old icehouse." Grat lit a fresh cigar. "I suppose the boy figures he's got himself a fast horse."

"That's silly," Mundy exclaimed. "You're not taking anything like that seriously, Grat?"

"What?" Collamore's tone was contemptuous. "You don't see anything green about me, do you? Of course it doesn't mean anything; but I suspect the Kid's in dead earnest about it. That's what I was trying to tell you; don't make fun of his horse."

"I guess it's a good tip at that," Joe admitted. "He takes himself pretty seriously. . . . I'll be seeing you, Grat."

Collamore favored him with a parting nod and returned to his interrupted contemplation of the flow of life along the street.

Johnnie was on his way down from Messenger's house, unaware that Mundy was looking for him, when he heard his name called as he was passing Rinehart's store. He turned to find Resa Kendrick smiling at him. He lifted his battered hat and felt strangely embarrassed. Resa had always been his friend at the Arrowhead.

"I'm glad to see you, Johnnie," she said. "The ranch hasn't been the same since you left." There was a warm friendliness in her voice that touched him. He was so used to seeing her in overalls that she seemed a little strange in her gray whipcord suit.

"It's nice of you to say that, Resa," he got out heavily. "You know why I left."

"We want you to come back to us, Johnnie. There won't be any more trouble over the dog. It's gone."

The Kid's face brightened.

"Somebody finally used a gun on that wolf, eh? Who was it, Resa?"

"Joe gave the dog away, Johnnie. He's sorry he lost his temper and slapped you. He drove me in today. He's looking you up before we go home. He's going to ask you to come back to your old job. . . . Please, Johnnie!" she pleaded as she saw his face cloud. "Meet him half-way, won't you?"

"I'm through with ranch work, Resa," the boy said

soberly. "I got a good job here in town. I'm workin' for Dan Messenger. If Mundy is sayin' he's sorry he banged me around, he's sayin' it because yore pa is makin' him say it. I'll never give him a chance to lay a hand on me ag'in."

Something in the depths of Resa Kendrick's hazel eyes said she admired his stand. But she felt obliged to defend her father's foreman.

"Banging you around, as you put it, was uncalled for. I wouldn't want you back if I thought anything like that was likely to be repeated. Joe knew the men hated the dog; he felt they were picking on it. It was unfortunate that when he boiled over it had to be with you. I refuse to believe it was just meanness on his part."

"That's because you think the best of everybody," the Kid said without retreating an inch. "I hope you never have to change yore opinion of him; but I can tell you he knows how to look out for himself; he's got some big ideas about where he's goin' to end up."

The girl's head went up and her mouth lost its long curve.

"Johnnie—what do you mean by that?" she demanded sharply. She surmised that she understood him perfectly.

The boy shook his head and scraped his scuffed boots.

"If you don't know, I better not tell you. Reckon he ain't foolin' Stark Tremaine."

This was being almost too frank for Resa. She laughed to cover her confusion.

"You needn't be troubled on that score," she said lightly. "Even a girl should be able to figure out some things for herself. I'm not going to urge you to change your mind but do think it over before you say no."

"There's nothin' to think over," the Kid declared doggedly. "If you see Mundy you can tell him not to waste his time lookin' me up."

They spoke a minute longer and the boy was turning away, when Mundy came across the street and called him back.

"I've been looking for you, Kid," he said, with attempted good-will. "Has Resa told you we want you to come back to Arrowhead?"

"Yeh," was the boy's muttered answer.

"Johnnie says he isn't interested," the girl explained. "He's found a job in town."

"That's foolish," Mundy declared patronizingly. "Working in town is all right in the winter, Johnnie, but don't tell me they can coop up an old ranch hand like you till the weather closes in. I was all wrong about ruffing you up; I was sorry for it the next day. If you'll give me the chance, I'll make it up to you some way. I felt so bad about losing my head that I got rid of the dog. There's no reason why we can't patch things up."

He stuck out his hand. The Kid ignored it.

"Why don't you put yore cards on the table, Mundy? I know why you want me back; Black Lightnin' has been brought in from the range and put on hard grain. The old man knows it's time to begin workin' him out a little."

"Sure!" Joe admitted readily. "There's no secret about that. The boss wants to put Black Lightning in your hands and have you stay with him till the race is over. He could get a boy from Green River. But he won't think of it; he wants you and nobody else. I don't blame him for feeling that way; you can top anything around here. You know, Kid, when Reb brought that big ink spot down from the high pasture and turned him into the Number Two corral, that horse kept on the move for an hour, looking for you. He misses you, sure enough."

This was an adroit argument, and it got the boy. Mundy tried to press it home.

"You know he can be mean when he wants to. But you always could do as you pleased with him. I guess a horse like that just picks out his man, and that's all there is to it."

"The two of us got along good together," Johnnie said simply. "Black Lightnin's all right. You can't git anywheres with him if you go at it hammer and tongs; he won't stand for that." He glanced at Resa. "You better tell that to whoever yore pa gits to ride him."

"Johnnie, is your decision as final as that?"

The Kid nodded firmly. "I ain't ridin' Black Lightnin'."

Mundy still had a trump or two to play, and he led them. Turning to Resa, he said, "After what I was told down the street, I didn't have much hope that we could make Johnnie see it our way. He isn't saying anything about it, but he's got his own horse. Rainbow Ripley bought him a mustang, and I hear it's looking pretty good."

"Who told you that?" the Kid demanded gruffly.

"Why, I saw Grat Collamore as I was passing the hotel. I happened to tell him I was looking for you. He warned me that if you find your horse really has something that you'd be riding for yourself this year, if you could scrape up the entrance fee."

"I can't believe it," Resa said. "Johnnie racing his own horse! Is it really true?"

"No one's heard me say anythin' about racin' him," the Kid answered. "And Mundy, you can tell Grat Collamore that what I'm doin' ain't none of his business."

"Grat wasn't talking out of turn," Joe argued. "Don't take it that way. Someone told him you had the horse. It doesn't mean anything to him. Maybe we can make it mean something—that's if you really think your bronc can run."

"Yeh?" the Kid queried suspiciously. "What do you mean?"

Joe played his ace.

"I was thinking you could fetch him out to the ranch and work him and Black Lightning together. It wouldn't cost you a penny for grain. We've got that measured half-mile; we could time you and keep things quiet. You've got five to six weeks to go yet. If your horse shows he can run, we'll chip in and put up the entrance money. You can ride Black Lightning in the stake race and be up on your own horse in the free-for-all."

The Kid had begun to shake his head.

"I'm doin' all right by myself, Mundy, and I ain't interested in any scheme like that. Talkin' about racin' a horse that ran wild on the desert and has never been shod is nonsense. Mebbe his hoofs won't hold a set of shoes.

Whatever he turns out to be, he gits all my time, not half of it. But I'll promise you one thing, Resa; I won't ride against Black Lightnin' on any other man's horse, no matter what I'm offered. I give you my word on that."

She expressed her thanks.

"I'll tell Father; I'm sure he'll appreciate it. . . . I guess there's nothing further to be said, Joe."

"No, I don't suppose there is!" Mundy jerked out angrily. "The stubborn little fool would sooner go hungry than come off his high perch. It's too bad I didn't knock a little sense into him while I was about it."

Resa stared him to silence.

"Knocking sense into fifteen-year-old boys is pretty low business for a man," she said chillingly. She nodded farewell to the Kid. "I wish you luck with your horse, Johnnie. And thanks for the advice you gave me."

She turned on her heel and was several steps away before Mundy caught up with her. The Kid stood there watching them go up the street. Resa's shoulders were stiff and uncompromising.

"Reckon she's gittin' wise to that gent!" he muttered solemnly.

On reaching the flats Johnnie went to the corral first. Champ saw him coming and nickered a greeting. The Kid looked the buckskin over carefully and then let him nuzzle him. This searching for a lump of sugar had become a game between them that both enjoyed.

"Here it is, Champ," the Kid announced, holding out the sweet. "Some folks are beginnin' to figger yo're goin' to turn out to be a race horse, mister. Mebbe they know what they're talking about."

For several days he had been packing the animal's hoofs in wet clay and binding it on with pieces of gunnysacking. The wrappings were dry again, and he got a bucket of water and soaked them. When he got to the cabin, he told his father he had met Resa and Mundy and what the Arrowhead foreman had had to say. Mr. Smiley wagged his head over it thoughtfully.

"Don't sound right to me, the foreman of a big outfit

spreadin' himself that-a-way. The more a man's got to say, the less truth you can look fer per word. In my time I knew every range boss from here half-way to Windy River. Mundy did more talkin' in a few minutes than them old ramrodders would have given out with in a month o' Sundays. Reckon Pike Kendrick sent him in with orders not to take no' fer an answer from you."

"I wasn't fooled by the way he tried to play up to me, Pappy. Reckon the next thing I can expect is to have the old man himself comin' after me. He'll git the same answer I gave Mundy. I'm sticking with Dan and Champ, and no one's changing my mind about it."

"That's right, Johnnie. I ain't got nuthin' in partic'lar ag'in Pike Kendrick—it's kinda ranch law fer an owner to side with his foreman in all disputes—but ridin' his hosses never put any meat in the pot for us. It's a steady job that keeps the money comin' in. The time you spend on Champ don't cost you nuthin'; and it's kinda comfortin' to sit here and know you got a hoss jest outside the door. Kinda makes you feel like you was somebody."

They had been living better recently and his position in regard to the horse had changed completely. There was a jar of jam on the table, where he sat finishing his lunch. He piled the jam so high on a slice of bread that raising it to his mouth without spilling it was a delicate operation. He smacked his lips over it.

"Never tasted no jam like that!" he declared. "That Mrs. Messenger is a fine woman, Johnnie. Whole strawberries in that jam. Taste jest like you'd plucked 'em right off the plant!"

He pushed away his empty plate and fumbled for his pipe and tobacco.

"A good woman can help a man a lot, Johnnie. There was a mess of them McFarland gals, five, six, at least. The old man didn't think much of the youngest one marryin' Dan. It turned out she did the best of all."

The Kid wasn't listening. He got up and started clearing away the table; he'd had his own lunch in the Messenger kitchen. Out of a moody silence, he said, "Reckon

I couldn't expect to keep folks from knowin' I was workin' Champ out in the evenin's, but I didn't know I was bein' watched. If there was a piece of good horse-flesh around, Collamore would make it his business to find out about it. I ain't let Champ out since the first night I rode him. I'm glad now I didn't. I don't want a lot of talk goin' around."

Mr. Smiley sucked unsuccessfully on his pipe and when he couldn't get it to draw asked the boy to get him a straw from the broom.

"Champ's yore hoss," he said, when the operation on the pipe was completed. "You don't have to keep him out of sight. If Rainbow was here, he'd tell you so; he took care of things like that when he made Pete give him a bill of sale. Nobody's puttin' anythin' over on him and Grumpy Gibbs. How long did they say they were goin' to be away this time?"

"Rip said he didn't know. That's the real reason I don't want folks watchin' every move I make; I want to be able to surprise him when he gits back. That's why I ain't been sayin' much even to Dan and Buck."

"Seems someone's bin doin' some talkin'," Mr. Smiley observed. "Jest gossip, I reckon; keepin' track of other folks' business is kinda the leadin' activity of this town. But you know Grat Collamore wouldn't be interested in Champ 'less he had reason to believe the hoss was goin' to upset all calculations about the race. You don't think Champ's that good, do you, Johnnie?"

"He can run, but I don't know how good he is," the Kid declared tensely. "I won't know till I give him a chance to show me. I'm goin' to keep his feet in clay for a few days more before I have Chris Hoeffler put a set of light shoes on him. When he gits used to wearin' 'em, I'll put him over the road and let him show me what he's got; and we'll do our workin' out just after dawn. If anybody wants to spy on us they'll have to git out purty early!"

CHAPTER 6

RAINBOW DID A THOROUGH JOB of smashing the saloon window. The shattered glass was still falling with its peculiarly chilling sound when several men popped out of the door, seeking an explanation. Inside, the noisy arguments and hilarity subsided for the moment as necks were craned toward the street. Surprise turned to amazement when Grumpy's .45 barked thunderously in the low-ceilinged room. Over the heads of the crowd Rip could now see him perched on the bar.

"Back over against the wall and stay put!" the little man growled. "There don't want to be no nonsense about this!"

The men found something written on his hard-bitten face that carried conviction. They backed away, some with their hands raised. Rainbow pushed past the several men at the door and moved along the bar until he stood just below Grump. Seeing them together snapped the lanky, slow-thinking Ferguson out of his trance.

"It's them dirty spies of Conroy's!" he bellowed. "We don't have to take no pushin' around from the snoopin' skunks! Pull 'em down, boys, and run 'em to hell outa of here!"

Bill Doxey and Torchy Wright, the two men who had passed the partners in front of the church, echoed his cry, and with two others started to rush the bar.

"Hold it!" Grumpy whipped out fiercely. "And keep yore mouths buttoned! My pardner and me are doin' all the talkin' here for a minit!"

It was no surprise to Rip to find every man in the barroom against them, and he included the owner of the saloon and his two bartenders, thanks to the shattered window and the interruption of business. He started to speak, only to be howled down. He waited before he tried again.

"You better hear what I've got to say," he rapped. "It'll open your eyes."

"Go get him, Bill!" Ferguson urged. "The gun is just a bluff!"

Doxey thought otherwise and was satisfied to stay where he was. "Let 'em wag their tongues, Ed," he growled. "We know what we'll hear from them. Who the hell will pay any attention to what they got to say?"

"We've got a man here that you'll pay some attention to," Rainbow answered him. "I don't mean you personally, Doxey; you and the rest of Strait's highbinders don't have to listen, but you men who're bound for Nevada will want to get an earful. . . . Joe! Come on in!" he called.

There was a pause, and the thought crossed his mind and Grumpy's that Pickens might have run out on them. Their anxiety was shortlived, for the storeroom door opened and Joe Pickens leaped up on the bar.

"It's Joe Pickens!" chorused half a dozen men.

"So some of you know me, eh?" Pickens flung back. He singled out Ed Ferguson, and his eyes blazed. "How about you, horseface? You ought to remember me, you double-crossing rat! And you, too, Doxey!"

"Better stop the name-calling and tell the men your story," Rip advised.

"Sure!" Pickens agreed. "And I got a story to tell you guys. I used to work on this job like you. Sam Strait shipped me up. He tipped me off that Ferguson would be looking out for me, just in case there might be a chance of better money somewhere else." Joe laughed harshly. "I'll say Ferguson looked out for me! I was here two weeks when he passed the word to about twenty-five of us that Sam had something out in Nevada at a dollar and a half a day and a bonus for the time we'd lose getting out there. And there was to be no second rake-off for him coming out of our pockets. Strait was just being a good guy; he liked us and he wanted to get us a break!"

The men were shifting about uneasily, some of them seeming to surmise what was coming. When Ferguson and his cohorts began to hoot and yell and make it impossible for Joe to continue, the crowd turned on them threateningly and they were silenced without any help from the partners.

Pickens stood there with a mocking laugh on his lips. All the bitterness he had been storing up for weeks was finding expression tonight.

"What I'm telling you sounds kinda familiar, don't it?" he jeered. "You suckers have been getting the same brand of bunk Ferguson handed me and my pals. I can tell you what you have ahead of you; I know; I been all through it. When you roll into Denver, you're going to have a nice new five-dollar bill put in your mitt. That's your bonus to cover the three days you'll lose getting out to that W. P. job. Good old Sam Strait, the poor man's friend! And then you'll be dumped out on the desert a couple mornings later, and what are you going to find? Are you going to get that dollar fifty a day? Sure, you're going to get it— for a week! That's when you get the bad news. It's a buck a day the rest of the way. . . . Wait a minute!" He shouted as a grumbling roar rose from the crowd. "Maybe you figure that was just a mistake. The guys you've been working with just laugh at you; they been through it, too; they tried to tell you what you had coming. What can you do about it? Who can poor saps like us make a squawk to? It's a hell of a long way to the next job—if you could find one. Your great friend Sam Strait and these lice have sold you out; but you can't do anything about it; you're stuck!"

"How much is Conroy payin' you for all this?" Ferguson cried.

"That's the answer!" Bill Doxey shouted at the men. "Ask him what he's getting out of this! Ask him for proof!"

"I'll give you all the proof you need!" Pickens cried in answer to that challenge. He whipped off his coat and shirt and showed the half-healed scars and welts on his back and told them the story of how he had returned to Denver to square accounts with Strait and what had happened to him.

Rip and Grumpy were powerless to stop what followed. The men seized Ferguson, Doxey and three others—there seemed to be no doubt in their minds as to who were Strait's agents—and ran them out into the street. News of what was happening had reached the other saloon and emptied it in a hurry. Aurora's town marshal tried to fight his way through the swarming crowd, in the center of which Ferguson and his handymen were being beaten to a pulp.

"Let me through!" the marshal shouted as fists continued their bone-crushing tattoo. "Yo're killin' those fellas!"

Petersen and half a hundred like him didn't intend to go that far, but they weren't to be stopped until they had the five men stretched in the dust. They dragged them to the creek then and flung them in, leaving it to the ice cold water to revive them before they drowned. Ferguson and the others crawled out on the far bank and painfully made their way up the stream in the direction of the camp, the crowd hooting at them derisively until they disappeared around a bend.

The partners and Joe Pickens had witnessed the proceedings from the doorway of the saloon. They had every reason to congratulate themselves on the way things had gone.

"It won't be necessary for us to say anythin' to Mike Moran about this," Grumpy declared, with a chuckle. "He'll get it as soon as he steps out of his tent tomorrow mornin'. He won't have to wire Denver for more men this week."

"It couldn't have worked out better from our end," said Rip. "Ferguson and his bunch are through. It'll take Strait a little time to get reorganized. I want to be around when he gets the news. We'll take the morning train out and shuck these duds as soon as we reach the city." He smiled at Pickens. "You must feel better, Joe; you did things up brown. Do you know what you're going to do now?"

"I'm going to strike Moran for a job. I don't know what I'm going to do about your twenty-five bucks; it's going to take me a long time to pay—"

"You've paid that back with interest already," Rainbow

interjected. "Forget about it. When I see Conroy I'll put in a boost for you that won't hurt you any. If it's possible to eat in Aurora at this time of night, let's find the spot."

The partners had nothing at camp that they were interested in claiming, and they decided to spend the night in town.

"You may find something in our suitcases that you can use," Rip told Pickens. "If there is, help yourself. We'll just curl up in a soft spot along the creek later on and let it go at that."

At seven-thirty the next morning they were on their way to Denver.

"Seems I'm gittin' so I can't take it no more," Grumpy complained. "I don't know whether it was the night air or it's just punishment for my sins, but I shore got a misery in my back this mornin'. When I git to Black Forks I'm goin' to do a lot of sittin' down, I promise you."

"I hope we can close this thing up in a few days; I'd like to be heading home, too," said Rainbow. "I was just wondering how Johnnie was getting along with his horse."

The little one grunted caustically. "You might better be askin' yoreself when they held his funeral." He winced as he shifted around on the seat. "The aches I got in me makes me feel sorry for the Kid. Wash Smiley could sue you for damages for putting that outlaw in the boy's hands!"

Rainbow realized Grumpy's chatter was not to be taken seriously. Through the car window, he gazed at the magnificent panorama of peaks and mountains.

"There's good stuff in that boy, Grump. I wish we could do something for him. Giving him that horse doesn't amount to anything; he ought to be in school instead of out fighting for a living. I'm going to see if the Judge can't do something."

"I don't know what," the little man commented. "It better not be anythin' in the way of help from the county; the Kid wouldn't take kindly to that. I'm afraid it'd slap him down awful hard even to suggest it."

"I'm sure it would," said Rip. "If you're going to help

him, you've got to do it without hurting his pride. . . . I hope this train doesn't leave the tracks. Not much ballast been put in along here."

"They've got a gang workin' north from the junction, I heard. Tell me, how's Ferguson goin' to git word to Strait? It's Sunday. He can't get a letter off; the post office will be closed. There won't be anyone around the depot either to take a telegram."

"I imagine he'll be on the next train. That'll give us time enough to get straightened out. Strait's going to howl when he hears what's happened. It'll certainly call for contact between him and the party for whom he's working. We'll have to watch every move he makes for a day or two. You wanted some sitting down. Chances are you'll have plenty of it to do."

"That part of it's all right," the little man grumbled. "It ain't likely this party will be comin' to Strait's office for any git-together."

"Not if he's one of Conroy's competitors."

"There's no if about it in my mind," said Grumpy. "When Conroy told us these other firms was all responsible people and good friends of his, I thought he might be wrong. The way things have shaped up doesn't seem to leave any doubt about it. We know this racket is costin' somebody some real dough. Who else but one of these so-called friends of his could be interested in goin' that far to hand him the works."

The tall man shook his head. "I can't give you an argument on that. The first thing for us to do is to rent an upstairs office in some building close enough to Strait's place so we can keep tabs on who comes and goes. We'll hire a carriage by the day and have it waiting below. If a hack rolls up to his door and he drives away, we'll be able to follow him."

They had no difficulty engaging a room for a week that promised to serve their purpose. They tipped the janitor a dollar and he produced a couple of dilapidated chairs. It was late Sunday afternoon by now. The street had a deserted look. After watching Strait's office for a few minutes and convincing themselves there was no one there, they changed clothes and walked up to the Albany and registered. A hot bath proved to be what Grumpy needed.

"Feel like I'm living ag'in," he declared. "I'm ready for dinner."

"We'll have it," Rip said, with a grin, "and if there's a good show in town, we'll take it in. I spoke to the porter about a carriage and told him to have it here at seven-thirty in the morning. We'll arrive at our office in style."

The current theatrical attractions were listed on a board in the lobby. The well-known actor, Guy Bates Post, a great Denver favorite, was at the Tabor Grand in "The Heir to the Hoorah."

"That ought to be good enough for us," Rainbow observed. "We'll stop at the cigar stand and have them reserve some seats."

With its good food and music, the Albany was a popular place on a Sunday evening, and the partners found the cafe well filled, though it was still early. Grumpy put on his gold-rimmed spectacles and picked up the menu as soon as they were seated. The only light in the restaurant was provided by the shaded lamps on the tables.

"You better do the orderin' if you can see to read what's on the card," the little man complained. "So dim in here I can't see nuthin'. Got this place dolled up like a lady's boodwar, with all these artificial vines and red lamps. A steak and some French fries will do for me."

Rip was facing the door. He was studying the menu, when the headwaiter hurried past, showing a man and woman to a table in the rear. The woman was young and pretty. Rip quickly raised the menu before his face as a screen; he had got a flash of the couple and recognized them instantly.

"Come on!" he snapped at Grumpy. "We're getting out of here. Don't waste any time asking why."

"Something wrong, gentlemen?" the startled waiter inquired.

Rip dropped a dollar on the table and started out. Grumpy overtook him in the lobby.

"What's the idea?" the latter demanded huffishly.

"Grump, that couple the head-waiter just took past our table—the woman is that good-looking girl who used to be Conroy's secretary. Do you know who's with her?"

"No!"

"Sam Strait."

"Then evidently she didn't git married, as you figgered, or she wouldn't be steppin' out with Strait. But what's so unusual about her bein' with that bird? I suppose he saw her in the office two or three times a week when she was workin' for Conroy and McCann and got acquainted with her. I don't think much of her judgment in runnin' around with him, but . . . Wait a second! Say, if Strait said anythin' to her about us, she could have told him who we are; she knows we worked for Conroy before."

"Undoubtedly that's what happened. But I'm sure we've stumbled on to something more important than that. Isn't it reasonable to suppose that when she left Conroy that she went to work for some other construction company? Now we catch her out with Strait. Don't you see how things hook up?"

"I'd have to be dumb if it didn't!" Grumpy removed his spectacles and returned them to the case, closing the lid with a sharp click. "We better have our dinner at the Brown Palace. How sure are you they didn't see us?"

"They didn't, Grump. It shouldn't be difficult to find what firm she's with now. When we do, we'll be close to winding things up. I'm trying to recall her name. There was one of those little name plates on her desk. . . . Miss—"

"Johnson, wasn't it?"

"That does it! Not Johnson, but Jensen. Miss Jensen!" With a twinkle in his gray eyes, Rip said, "It's started out to be a very pleasant evening."

"Yeh, if we don't find Strait and the gal sittin' next to us in the theatre."

"We'll make sure we don't run into them," Rip said. "We'll be through with dinner before they are. We'll walk back to the Albany and see what they do when they come out. If they go to the opera house, we'll have to pass up the show."

When they returned to the hotel, they watched both entrances. It was almost eight o'clock before Strait and the Jensen girl came out. They turned into Seventeenth Street and walked away from the business district. After following them some blocks, the partners saw them enter one of Denver's fashionable apartment houses.

"This Burdick Court is purty sweel quarters for a gal in her circumstances," Grumpy commented.

"I don't know," Rainbow countered. "Miss Jensen's circumstances may surprise us. I suspect she is doing very well for herself. Let's get back down-town; Strait's evidently not taking her to the theatre this evening."

They walked away rapidly.

"Is it yore idea that the gal is bein' used as the go-between?" the little one questioned as they swung along. Rainbow nodded.

"I can't think anything else until the evidence shows I'm mistaken. If you'll stretch your legs a little more, we'll just about catch the curtain."

CHAPTER 7

THERE WAS A TANG IN THE AIR these mornings that told the Kid summer was definitely gone. To the north, the towering peaks of the Solomons seemed nearer. Over the plains, hung a blue autumnal haze. Most of the idling ranch hands had disappeared from their haunts along the main street of Black Forks. The boy knew that hay was being put up and cattle being worked down from the high places.

Fall was the pleasantest time of the year on the range. Old memories tugged at Johnnie. He knew it wouldn't be long before the aspens above Singing Creek would be turning yellow. Any day now the Arrowhead chuck wagon would be run out of the shed and greased and made ready for the round-up. He had "rode" the wagon the previous year and rustled wood for big Elmer, the round-up cook, at whose dexterity and skill he had never ceased to marvel. He thought of Reb Justin, Bret Failes and Happy Sherdell, his favorites among the Arrowhead crew.

"I'd shore like to see 'em," he muttered to himself, as he went to the creek for water for Champ. "The country must be real purty now, up to'ards Squaw Butte. I could put away a stack of Elmer's flapjacks and a pan of bacon this mornin'. I shore could!"

And yet when he reached the corral and Champ nickered a greeting, the Kid knew he wouldn't trade his present lot for a dozen jobs on Arrowhead. As though his nostalgic thoughts had held some disloyalty to the big buckskin, he said, "A fella can't help thinkin' back sometimes, Champ, but I don't really mind not goin' out with the wagon; I got you, and that's all that matters. I'm goin' to git you a set of shoes this afternoon, and you ain't going to like it, big fella. No horse does for the first time. But it won't hurt; I'll see that Chris is extry careful with you."

He was wetting down the sidewalk, the rest of his daily chores finished, when Messenger came around the corner. He had his usual friendly good morning for the boy.

"You're finishing up early, Johnnie."

"Mrs. Messenger wants me to give her a hand transplantin' some flowers. I figgered I'd git up to the house a little ahead of time, Mr. Messenger."

Dan smiled. "I didn't think she'd let anyone touch her peonies."

He was well pleased with the way the boy did his work. He had wisely refrained from giving him too much praise, however, feeling Johnnie neither wanted nor would be helped by any coddling.

"You didn't happen to see Buck Rainsford ride by?" Messenger questioned. He took it for granted that the Kid knew word had reached town during the night that a man had been killed at the stage station in Tipstone Valley and that the sheriff had left for the scene of the shooting at once.

"He jogged by about twenty minutes ago," Johnnie answered.

"Did you talk to him?"

"No, he seemed to be in a hurry. He looked purty dusty. . . . Is there anything wrong?"

"Steve Ellis was killed last night."

The Kid straightened up, his eyes wide and incredulous.

"Steve?" he burst out excitedly. "Who got him, Mr. Messenger?"

"According to the story Buck got last night, Joe Mundy shot him. That may not be correct. I'll run up and look at the mail and go over to the courthouse then. I wouldn't let this break me up if I were you, Johnnie. I know you liked Steve; most everyone did. But he would drink too much at times. I presume that was the trouble last night."

"He was a good friend of mine," the Kid said tensely. He choked back his emotion and his young face turned hard and bitter. "There wasn't nothin' mean in Steve. He'd give you his shirt if you needed it. If he drank too much sometimes, it wasn't often. It'd take a yellow-livered skunk like Mundy to pick trouble with him."

"It'll be time enough to express an opinion when we know the details," said Dan. "If you're finished, go up to the house; I'll see Buck."

The Kid nodded his head.

"I'll go up as soon as I git done with the sidewalk. I bet Mundy doesn't git away with this. Somebody will take it up."

Messenger let it pass without comment, but he was secretly of the same opinion as Johnnie. Steve Ellis had been born and raised in the Black Forks country. He had always had friends, even when he didn't have much of anything else. For the past three years he had managed to squeeze a living out of a small cow ranch on the eastern slope of Tipstone Valley.

Dan met the sheriff as the latter came out of the district attorney's office.

"I've just been in talkin' things over with Ashforth," Buck volunteered. "He agrees with me that it would be foolish to try to indict Mundy. He'd plead self-defense and the Grand Jury wouldn't hold him."

"Then it *was* Mundy who shot Steve," Messenger said. "What led up to it, Buck?"

"Mundy and a couple Arrowhead riders stopped at the station for a drink. Steve was there. He'd had a few. The two punchers, Pasco and Rocky Lesant, claim he was drunk. Cain was behind the bar. He ain't so sure Steve was drunk, but says he'd been drinkin'. The argument started over that dog Mundy owned, that one that chewed up the Kid. I guess it was half wolf. It seems Mundy gave it to Dad Early, the Government hunter. Steve stops at Dad's cabin a couple of days ago and the dog snaps it chain and lunges at him. He promptly slaps a slug into it. Mundy admits that killin' the dog made him sore, but he says he held in. Steve begins ridin' him then about givin' the Kid a beatin'. Their stories all agree that when the two of 'em finally went for their guns that Steve drew first. He fired a shot, all right. I don't know whether he meant it or was just tryin' to put the crawl on Mundy."

"Mundy nailed him, of course," Dan's tone was sober. "That shot of Steve's—where did it land, Buck?"

"I dug the slug out of the ceilin'." Rainsford shook his head. "Steve Ellis was awful neat with a six-gun. Drunk or sober, it's hard for me to believe he'd be that wild if he shot first."

"Me, too," Dan declared. "This won't be the end of it, Buck. I agree with Johnnie on that."

"The Kid knows about it, eh?"

"He doesn't know the argument centered around him." Dan shook his head. "I don't like that part of it at all. It could very easily throw the boy off balance."

"I don't believe it will," Buck drawled. "The Kid was thinkin' of Stark Tremaine, no doubt; Stark was Steve's best friend. I've caught a hint here and there for some time that there'd be a face-up between them some day. I don't know why some people should always be harpin' on it. Mundy's always been too cocky for me, but I figger you can like him or leave him alone. He's made Pike a good man, and this is the first time he's been mixed up in anythin' that doesn't look right."

Messenger regarded him carefully for a moment.

"You say you don't know why the talk got started. I think you do, Buck; you don't miss many tricks. You were at the dance at the Tipstone school this spring. You saw enough to tell you what stands between them."

Rainsford looked up from beneath his shaggy brows.

"Resa Kendrick?"

"That's reason enough."

Rainsford pulled down the corners of his mouth.

"I give her credit for too much sense to be caught in the middle of anythin' like that. You better have a talk with the Kid and straighten things out in his mind. Ordinarily, I'd consider it a mistake to make too much over his horse—he's got his hopes up purty high as it is—but it might be the thing to do right now. . . . Have you been out on the flats yet?"

"I finally got down last evening. I'd put it off for the very reason you mention. Looks never made a fast horse, but I've got to admit I was a little surprised at what Johnnie had to show me. The stallion is a big, strong horse. I suspect there's very little mustang blood in him."

"Did the Kid run him for you?"

"No, he's got Champ's feet plastered with clay. He's going to have him shod this afternoon. The stallion is four years old. Without trying to sound discouraging, I pointed out to Johnnie that it was asking a lot to expect a horse that had been running wild for a long time to face a crowd and band music and all the other excitement of a race. We talked it over, and I suggested that it might be wise for him to make his plans on a long range basis and get Champ ready for next year and not to enter him this fall."

"What was his answer to that?" Buck questioned.

"It stopped me." Dan grinned. "He told me that seeing

as how Rainbow had bought the horse for him that he'd have to be guided by whatever Ripley had to say. I couldn't quarrel with that, Buck."

"No. We'll have to git hold of Rip as soon as he shows up. I'm convinced the Kid is playin' with a cold deck. If he had the entrance money and Champ was the fastest thing on four legs in the state of Wyomin', he still wouldn't have a chance of gittin' him to the post. And the more chance he would seem to have of takin' the race, the less chance he'll have to git in it. You know Pike Kendrick will see to it that the horse is ruled off the minute it begins actin' up. The thing for us to do is let the Kid down as easy as we can."

Johnnie took Champ to the blacksmith shop that afternoon as he had planned. Dan had had a long talk with him. Knowing that on his account, as he viewed it, laughing Steve Ellis lay dead in Tipstone Valley, was a bitter load for him to bear. His hatred of Joe Mundy now burned with a fierce, implacable flame. Without intending any disparagement of Buck Rainsford's ability, he wished Rainbow and Grumpy were there that they might get to the truth of what had happened in the saloon at the Tipstone station. He refused to believe anything but that Mundy had wantonly killed Steve and made it look otherwise. Of all the Arrowhead crew, Tony Pasco and Rocky Lesant were chummy with Mundy. He felt they'd back him up in any move he made. As for Ike Cain, who ran the station, he was a worthless blackleg, distrusted and despised by all honest men.

The blacksmith shop was a popular hangout. The talk there was all of the shooting. The boy's arrival provided the loafers with an opportunity to draw him out. The Kid turned on them angrily.

"I ain't got nothin' to say," he growled. "I came here to git a horse shod, not to do any gabbin'!"

Champ objected to being led in. Hoeffler offered to give him a hand. Johnnie said no.

"I'll do better myself, Chris. I'll git him in if you'll make these fellas clear out."

Hoeffler asked the three men to step outside. After they had moved back to the road Johnnie quieted the horse and got him through the wide doors. The blacksmith snapped the straps into the halter rings. He regarded Champ with scowling anxiety as he began to rear and kick. There was some free advice from the little audience, now looking on from the entrance to the shop.

"I'll have to hobble him, Johnnie, and use the sling," Chris declared. "I won't be able to get near him if I don't."

"All right," the boy agreed. "Just don't be rough with him. I'll hobble him for you."

The hobble harness was an ingenious arrangement of leather straps that could be adjusted to fetter three of a horse's four legs at all times, enabling the blacksmith to work around a fractious animal with comparative safety. Hoeffler always claimed it was his own invention. Johnnie had often seen it used, and before Champ realized what he was in for, he was securely trussed up. It was a different matter when it came to lifting his right hind leg into the sling. But Chris Hoeffler was a determined German. He didn't weigh over a hundred and sixty pounds; a tough, wiry man whose feats of strength matched those of men almost twice his size. He finally got the horse's leg in his lap and began to pare the hoof. The Kid watched every move.

"How does it look, Chris?" He knew how much depended on Hoeffler's answer.

"Looks purty good. A little dry but no deep cracks, Johnnie."

"Gosh, that's good!" the boy exclaimed. "I been worried about his hoofs. Reckon the clay helped."

When the blacksmith tried to set the first shoe, Champ upset him and sent his kit flying. The Kid grabbed the head-stall and hung on as the big horse reared, afraid that Champ would throw himself and break a leg.

Hoeffler was upset three times before he got the shoe nailed on. He began to get mad, and it didn't make things easier for him. He got up, rubbing a skinned elbow. But for his boast that he had never seen the horse he couldn't shoe, he would have quit.

"He's a man-killer, Chris," someone said from the doorway. "If he ever breaks those hobbles, he'll kick the daylights out of you."

Grat Collamore had joined the little group of onlookers. The Kid recognized his voice before he caught a glimpse of him, and all of his pent up emotion exploded.

"Nobody's askin' for yore put-in, Collamore!" he lashed out angrily. "If you've got any advice to hand out, give it to yore friend Mundy; he'll be needin' it!"

Referring to Mundy as his friend puzzled Grat, who was in no danger of losing his temper, for his acquaintance with Arrowhead's foreman was as casual as with a hundred other men. The boy's feeling against the man needed no explanation, however.

"Why are you jumping down my throat, Johnnie? If Chris wants to fight that devil, that's his business; but it's time somebody opened your eyes."

"Yeh?" was the boy's contemptuous retort. "I got my eyes open!"

"Not according to what I hear. You're having a wonderful dream, but it's just a dream. You ought to know better than to think you can pit that animal against Black Lightning, the Chief and three or four others I can name."

The boy drew himself up tensely. "I'm glad you think so poorly of Champ! That suits me fine!"

"It ain't a question of what I think, Johnnie. Arentz and the other rodeo officials won't take a chance on him. They're not going to risk having things bungled up—maybe an accident. You could enter him in the wild horse race." Collamore chuckled. "If he didn't start running around the track the wrong way, you might win it."

It drew a round of laughter from the group in the doorway. Johnny faced them defiantly, the blood draining away from his face as he took their quips.

"If you've had yore fun why don't you move on?" he

blazed. "You ain't interested in my horse, so keep yore mouths shut!"

"I'm interested to the extent of fifty dollars," said Collamore. "I'd take him off your hands at that figure, or you can keep him if you'll agree to stay away from the rodeo. It'll be worth that much to me just to know you're not going to scramble up things so a man can't lay a bet intelligently."

That Collamore could make such an offer in all seriousness stunned the Kid, and the best answer he could manage was a contemptuous, if feeble, laugh. Hoeffler came to the boy's rescue.

"It ain't right to pick on the Kid like that and hurt his feelin's," he protested.

"I wisht somebody'd hurt my feelin's by offerin' me fifty dollars for a no-account crow-bait," one of the men cackled to the laughter of his companions.

"Yo're right, Milt; Grat's bein' real gen'rous!" another declared with mock gravity that made the Kid squirm. "Fifty dollars is a fancy price for hoss meat."

CHAPTER 8

UNNOTICED, STARK TREMAINE CAME DOWN the path outside the blacksmith shop as Johnnie faced his tormentors. His happy, carefree smile was missing today.

A few strides brought him to the door. He jerked a nod at the boy and ran his eye over Collamore and the others, in no doubt as to what had been going on.

"What seems to be the trouble here?" Tremaine asked quietly. "Have they been throwing the prod into you, Kid?"

"They're razzin' me and my horse. But I can take it." The boy's tone reflected his recovered confidence.

Tremaine's attention focused on Grat Collamore.

"I know it doesn't take much to amuse men like Milt

Tansy; but I wouldn't expect to catch you making game of a boy, Grat," he said, his voice deceivingly free of anger.

"I don't know where the Kid gets it, Tremaine, but he has the idea that I'm thick with Mundy. I did see him the last time he was in town. I was sitting on the hotel veranda when he passed. He told me he was looking for Johnnie; that Pike wanted him to ride Black Lightning. I told him the boy had a horse of his own and wasn't likely to be interested in going back to Arrowhead. Out of that the Kid seems to have got the idea that I'm against him. I don't want to see him attempt to race this horse. But strictly on my own account. I don't want to see a half broken horse that was running wild on the desert only a month ago brought into any race on which I'm making book. I don't think it's any kindness to the Kid to string him along. I told him frankly I'd give him fifty dollars for his horse and he could keep him if he'd promise not to try to enter him."

"That's straight from the shoulder, at least," said Stark, "though it seems a little early to be talking of buying the Kid off. I don't know what he's got in the way of a horse; this is the first time I've seen it."

He looked Champ over hurriedly. Hoeffler had finished with another shoe and was trying to get the animal's left hind leg into the sling and having a hard time of it. Tremaine turned to the Kid.

"Does Grat's proposition interest you, Johnnie?"

"Not for two seconds! He's puttin' words in my mouth when he talks about me racin' this horse. I ain't said nothin' of the kind."

"Shucks, Johnnie, it don't take a fortune-teller to figure out what you've got on your mind," Collamore declared. "You don't have to give me an answer this afternoon; think my proposition over."

"I got nothin' to think over. You ought to have sense enough to know. I wouldn't let anybody put up the entrance money for me unless my horse was ready. It ain't that yo're worryin' about. What you don't want is a dark horse in the race. If I'm ruled off it won't be for no other reason."

Grat shrugged his beefy shoulders.

"I won't argue with you, Kid, but whatever happens, you'll get a reasonably square deal from me."

With a parting nod to Tremaine, he turned down the path. The former leveled his eyes at Milt Tansy and the other two and they took the hint and followed Collamore.

"I'll see if I can't give you a hand, Chris," Tremaine said. "You take Champ's head and calm him down a little, Johnnie."

Even with some of the distractions removed the big horse fought every minute until Hoeffler was finished.

"That was as tough a job as I ever tackled," Chris declared, rubbing his bruises. "I'm afraid he'll raise hell when I drop the hobbles. I don't know whether the Kid will be able to hold him or not. You better lead him out, Tremaine."

"I can handle him," the boy insisted. "He knows me."

After a bad few minutes the Kid got the horse out of the shop.

"You can walk him home all right," Tremaine told him. "I've got a little business with Chris. When I finish, I'll get my bronc and ride down to the flats. There's something I want to say to you."

Champ didn't like the feel of his new shoes, but the wild light in his eyes began to fade and he permitted the boy to lead him down the street. By the time they reached the flats the stallion was moving along without giving any trouble. The Kid turned him into the corral. After dashing around the enclosure for several minutes and voicing his disgust in a series of angry snorts, he rolled in the dust and tried to kick off the offending shoes.

Johnnie gazed at him fondly.

"You got to git used to them, Champ. In a day or two you won't know you got 'em on."

When Tremaine arrived, he stopped at the cabin and said hello to Mr. Smiley. He continued on to the corral then, where the Kid stood, waiting.

"Your father knew Steve, but I didn't say anything to him about what happened," he explained. "I suppose the *Gazette* will be full of it this afternoon."

What he had to say about the shooting added little to the story Rainsford had brought in. Shortly before midnight someone had brought the news to Double Diamond. He said he and most of the crew had gone up to Tipstone at once.

"Steve had his faults, but a man couldn't ask for a better friend. We buried him this morning after the coroner got there. We placed him high up among the cedars on Sentinel Mountain where he'll have a lot of room and the wind will keep the grass stirring around him."

The Kid bit his lips.

"He'll appreciate that. . . . Does Mundy's story sound all right to you?"

The Double Diamond man shook his head.

"It sounds fishy to me, too," Johnnie said thinly. He studied his boots for a moment. "What are you goin' to do about it, Stark?"

"I'm not going to forget it," was the grim response. "We may never know exactly what happened, but usually these things come out. In the meantime, don't get the idea that any part of this is your quarrel."

"Is that what you had to tell me?"

Tremaine nodded.

"I know Steve was throwing it into Mundy about what he'd done to you. But they didn't like each other and they could have rowed just as easily about something else. The less you have to say about Joe Mundy the better off you'll be."

It was almost identical with the advice Messenger had given the boy.

"I got good reason to hate Mundy, and I do," Johnnie said with his old man's soberness. "But I won't have no trouble with him if he'll leave me alone."

Tremaine's gaze sharpened.

"Why do you say that? What makes you think he'll come at you?"

The Kid shrugged his thin shoulders and shook his head.

"I don't know. I crossed him, and you see what's come of it. If I know Joe Mundy, he figgers he's got a score to settle with me. I suppose Resa told you Rip had given me the horse."

"Yes, she did, and she said something that you'd do well to remember; and that is not to get your sights trained too high on Champ. I know you love horses, and I can see what he means to you. It'd be wonderful if he turned out to be a champion; but you can be happy with him without that."

"Shore," the Kid muttered weightily. "I'm jest hopin'—that's all. Other people can have a horse without causin' a lot of talk; I don't know why I can't."

"You won the stake race last year and finished second the year before; that's why. Think of it that way and get the chip off your shoulder. I've got to be running along. If you get the chance, let me know how things go with you."

The Kid offered to walk back to the road with him. They had just passed the cabin when they saw a heavy-set, florid faced man striding toward them.

"Pike Kendrick!" the Kid exclaimed under his breath. "I been expectin' him! You wait, Stark, and hear what he's got to say."

There was an air of authority, as well as prosperity about the gray-haired owner of Arrowhead. His hand-made boots and tailored clothes were the best that money could buy. He was annoyed to find Tremaine there, but save for a pulling down of his upper lip that caused his flowing mustache to rise, he gave no sign of it. He expressed his regret over Steve Ellis.

"I'm sorry it happened, but I couldn't ask my foreman not to defend himself."

"If you don't mind, Mr. Kendrick, I'd rather not discuss it," said Stark.

"There's no more that needs to be said," old Pike returned with his usual brusqueness. He fastened his eyes on the boy. "Johnnie, I don't want any more of this foolish-ness! I'm on my way over to Green River. If I can't make a deal with you, I'm goin' to get me a boy over there. I don't care whether you come out to the ranch or not, if that's what is stickin' in your craw. I know you don't get along with Mundy. But that's neither here nor there. I'm willin' to bring Black Lightnin' into town. I'll arrange with Arentz so you can work the horse at the rodeo grounds. If you win the race, I'll give you a hundred dollars. You and your pa can use a hundred; it'll keep you in grub all winter."

Tremaine frowned. Kendrick's offer was generous enough, but trading on the boy's poverty seemed a mean advantage to take.

If the Kid hesitated over his answer it wasn't because there was any uncertainty in his mind. But Kendrick was a big man in Johnnie's small world, and having leaped to do his bidding a thousand and one times had left its impression and he found it anything but easy to defy him.

"It shouldn't take you all afternoon to say yes or no!" Pike snapped impatiently.

"I don't like to let you down, Mr. Kendrick," the boy told him, "but I got to say no."

The old cowman's face reddened with anger and his mustache bristled.

"That's gratitude for you!" he snorted sarcastically. "Of all the nonsense I ever heard, this takes the cake!"

His outburst brought the boy's father to the door. Mr. Smiley shaded his eyes with his hand. "Is that you, Pike?" he called.

"Yes, Wash! Where does this boy of yours get the idiotic idea he's got somethin' fast enough to put in the race? Where is this horse? I want to have a look at him!"

Mr. Smiley took exception to this high-handed attitude, and he was not beyond giving Kendrick a dig.

"Take him down to the corral, Johnnie, and let him have a good look," he cackled. "Mebbe you can show him sunthin' that'll fetch him down off his high hoss."

Tremaine went back to the corral with the Kid and

Kendrick. The latter gave vent to a sharp grunt of surprise on catching sight of Champ.

"That's strange," he muttered to himself.

He walked around the corral, viewing the horse from every angle. His surprise faded and his eyes brightened with an obscure interest.

"What seems to be the trouble, Mr. Kendrick?" Tremaine inquired when he saw Pike nod, as though convinced of the correctness of what he was thinking. "You act as though you'd seen this horse before."

"I haven't anythin' to say—not now!"

The cowman's tone was curt and ominous. The Kid felt a shiver run down his spine.

"You never saw him before," he burst out hotly. "You can't pull no bluff like that on me! Mustang Pete trapped him way out beyond Sioux Rocks, and there ain't no marks on him!"

"I don't care where he was runnin'," Kendrick responded gruffly. "As for the absence of a brand, that don't mean a thing; a man brands his livestock for his convenience; the law don't require you to do it. But I've seen enough!"

He walked back toward the road rapidly and left Johnnie and Tremaine standing there. For all of his bold front, the boy had been shaken.

"His talk about given' me a hundred dollars was all wind; he had this thing planned out before he showed up! He's goin' to try some trick to take Champ away from me."

"I don't believe he'll succeed, but I agree that he'll try." Tremaine was not taking the incident lightly. "You talk to Dan Messenger; he can tell you what your rights are. I wouldn't lose any time about it, Johnnie. Pike Kendrick is usually a fair and honorable man, but not where a race is concerned. He'd rather have Black Lightning come in a winner than show a profit on Arrowhead."

CHAPTER 9

THOUGH RAINBOW AND GRUMPY ARRIVED at the shabby office from which they proposed to keep Strait's headquarters under surveillance at an early hour, they had not been at the windows more than a few minutes when they saw Ed Ferguson trying the door. Unable to get in, he began pacing back and forth in front of the building, his impatience obvious.

"He's boilin' over," Grumpy observed. "Reckon he ain't got to Strait with his bad news as yet."

"That would be my guess," said Rip.

Ferguson was joined shortly by Doxey and one of the others who had come to grief at Aurora. They kept glancing up the street in the direction from which they expected Strait to appear.

Rainbow pulled out his watch.

"It's eight o'clock. He ought to be showing up soon."

"Here he comes now, Rip. Watch this. It ought to be good!"

Strait lost his swagger the second he caught sight of Ferguson. He quickened his step, and even at a distance the partners could see his rocky face tightening with mingled wrath and anxiety.

Grumpy raised the window, but he and Rip were unable to catch a word of what followed. That was hardly necessary, however, for Strait's angry gestures and the hang-dog protestations of his men spoke for themselves. He was so beside himself that when he turned to the door, he had trouble getting the key into the lock.

"He acts to me like he knew the bottom had dropped out of the rain barrel," Grumpy declared with satisfaction. Pat Guffey crossed the street and pushed into the office as the little one was speaking. "Strait's got his right-hand man with him now, Rip. They can have a real pow-wow."

"Strait's the only one in there that I'm interested in," Rainbow remarked. "He'll make some move this morning, and he's not likely to do it by telephone. If something doesn't break by noon, I'm going to leave you here and try to get a line on the Jensen girl."

They didn't have to wait long for action. It was not yet nine o'clock when Strait hurried out and turned up the street. The hack the partners had hired was waiting below.

"You climb into it, Grump, and keep him in sight," Rip directed. "I'll follow him on foot."

He ran down the stairs, and before he reached the corner was only a few yards back of Strait. The latter turned to the left at the Albany. After several blocks, the man's destination became almost a certainty in Rainbow's mind. With a quiet, residential street opening before him, he slowed his pace and permitted Strait to draw further ahead.

The little one had been as quick as Rip to surmise that Strait was bound for the apartment house they had seen him enter with the girl the previous evening. Though he had the driver hold his team to a walk, he was almost abreast of Ripley when their man did the expected and turned into Burdick Court.

"You better drive right past the place for a hundred yards or so before you stop," Rainbow advised from the sidewalk. "I'll be along in a few minutes."

Having allowed Strait time enough to get upstairs, Rip walked into the building and pretended to be writing down the names on the mail boxes. He found the one he was seeking: Miss Celia Jensen, Apartment H. A uniformed houseman caught him at the boxes. "Who are you looking for?" he asked.

"Just getting names for the new directory," was Rainbow's ready excuse. "I suppose most of these tenants are new."

"Only one or two. We seldom have a vacancy."

Rainbow glanced at the boxes. "Some of these names are new to me. I don't remember Miss Jensen."

"She's been with us three years," the houseman volunteered.

It was a surprising bit of information. Ripley greeted it with a dissembling laugh. "Can't trust my memory any more," he said as he walked out.

Obviously, if Celia Jensen had been a resident of Burdick Court for three years, she had lived there during the time she had been employed by Conroy and McCann. It had inferences and connotations that made Rainbow revise some of his deductions.

Grumpy saw him coming and opened the carriage door.

"I had a little luck," Rip told him. "Miss Jensen has been living in that swank apartment house for three years. That rules out any idea she owes her present prosperity to a new job."

"Wal!" Grumpy declared pointedly. "That puts a different face on things. She ain't workin' for any construction company. We've got the answer to this riddle right at our finger tips if we'll just reach out and grab it."

"What do you suggest?" Rip asked.

"I'm for bustin' up there and findin' out just who Strait rushed out here to meet. That'll settle it. We won't find out whose money is behind that gal by sittin' in this hack."

"If we went up to Miss Jensen's apartment it would be just a case of chasing the ducks off the pond." Rainbow leaned back on the cushions and stretched his long legs. His gray eyes were thoughtful. "I'm not so sure there'll be a third party to the conference. The feeling grows in me that this hurried get-together is between Miss Celia Jensen and Sam Strait, and no one else. He knows the jig is up and that he's got to talk fast if he hopes to get another handout before the purse strings close. He couldn't have much hope of talking a man into coming through with more money. It would be different if he were dealing with a woman who was going all out to smash a man's business."

Grumpy's head came up. "Good grief," he growled, "are you tryin' to tell me this Jensen gal is responsible for all the trouble Conroy and McCann have been runnin' into?"

"It's a convincing explanation to me," said Rip.

The little man shook his head. "I can't say it ain't. A woman will go a long ways to square a grudge. But whose money is she usin'?"

"It could be Conroy's. She might have been a lot more to him than merely his secretary. All this is only a hunch. But we've played longer shots and had them stand up. Our best bet right now is to stick with Strait and see if we can't pick up something that will tend to confirm what we're thinking. We'll go to Conroy then and get his side of it. I don't imagine he'll relish having us delving into his private life, but if that's the way the cat is going to jump, we'll have to play it accordingly."

They had a long wait before they saw Strait emerge from the Burdick Court apartments. He turned back the way he had come. The partners gave him a safe start and then followed easily in the hack. When Strait was within a block of his office, he stepped into a bank.

"He must have made a touch," Grumpy asserted.

As soon as they were past the bank Rainbow told the driver to stop.

"You wait here, Grump; I'm going in. I'd like to see the check he's cashing."

Strait was standing at one of the customers' desks in the center of the room when Rip stepped in. He was endorsing a check. Rainbow picked up a pen and deposit slip at another desk and kept his head lowered until Strait went up to a teller's window. A glance at the check he presented satisfied the young man behind the wicket, who proceeded to cash it.

It was evidence enough that Strait had been here before. Of greater interest to Ripley, however, was the fact that the check that had just been presented was a personal one, its dimensions leaving no doubt but what it had come from a pocket-size book. Being familiar with the rules of most reputable banks, the tall man realized that only an astute move would enable him to discover on whose account the paper had been drawn. Several years back, when Grumpy and he had been handling a matter for the Rocky Mountain Short Line, Tom Street, the general manager of the railroad, had brought him into the bank and introduced him to Mr. Carpenter, one of its vice presidents. It suggested an approach, and after Strait had left, Rainbow had himself directed to the gentleman's office.

Carpenter recalled having met him.

"I remember the talk we had very clearly, Mr. Ripley. What can I do for you?"

"Do you know Sam Strait, the labor contractor?" Rainbow inquired.

"I know who he is. He carries a small account with us. Has this anything to do with the Short Line?"

"Indirectly. Strait cashed a sizeable check on Miss Celia Jensen's account a few minutes ago. I'm not making any accusations, but I think you'd be wise to examine her signature."

This was sheer bluff. Rainbow realized that if the long chance he was taking failed him he'd be hard put to find a way out.

Carpenter used the telephone. An assistant cashier appeared with the check and Miss Jensen's identification card a few minutes later. Carpenter compared the signatures carefully.

"I'm afraid you're mistaken, Mr. Ripley," he said. "The signature on this check is all right."

He didn't offer to show it to Rainbow. But that wasn't important; the latter had got the information he wanted.

"It was just a tip that I thought was worth running down," he said. "I'm sorry I bothered you."

Grumpy noticed the satisfied look on his partner's face when he saw him coming. Rip gave the driver the address of the building in which the Conroy and McCann offices were located.

"Somethin' clicked for you," the little one declared.

"In a big way, Grump! If Dan Conroy will open up to us, we can be on the Union Pacific this evening, bound for home."

What he had to say about the check satisfied Grumpy that the end of the case was in sight.

"When the facts get noised around it'll put Sam Strait

out of business. None of these big construction outfits will have anythin' to do with him. But it'll leave Conroy with a headache. I don't see how he can bring criminal proceedin's against either the gal or Strait."

"What he does is not our worry," said Rip. "We can pay off this hackman; we don't need him any longer."

When they got upstairs, they had to wait twenty minutes or longer before Conroy could see them.

"I understand you've been busy," he told them. "Moran wired me this morning. Have you got a line yet on who's behind Sam Strait?"

"Yes, and it's going to surprise you," Rip answered. "You can charge this experience up to an old employe of yours—Miss Celia Jensen."

"What?" Conroy gasped, half rising in his chair. Ashenfaced, he stared at the partners in stunned amazement for a long moment and then sank back with a groan. Suddenly he popped to his feet and closed and locked the door. "I wasn't prepared for anything like this," he got out uncertainly as he returned to his desk. "What proof have you got, Ripley?"

"Suppose we clear up one or two things before we tell you what we've learned," Rip countered. "I realize this is very personal. You know Strait has been well paid for his efforts. Have you any reason to believe that Miss Jensen is in a financial position to have supplied the money?"

"Yes," Conroy gulped. "A man does some damned foolish things!"

"Can you think of some reason she might have had for going out to smash you?"

"Reason, Ripley?" Conroy threw up his hands hopelessly. "What reason does a vindictive woman need? She could think up a hundred! Good heaven's man, don't keep me waiting! What do you know?"

"We better start at the beginnin'," Grumpy spoke up. "It didn't take us long to discover where Strait fitted into the picture. We knew he wasn't spendin' his own money, but it wasn't until this mornin' that we found out where it was comin' from."

It did not take them long to acquaint Conroy with the facts at their command. The latter mopped his perspiring brow.

"I'll drive Sam Strait out of this town for his part in this dirty business!" he declared, his voice rough and bitter. "It's hard to estimate how much the delays have cost us on the Short Line job, but we can squeeze through now. I'm certainly indebted to you gentlemen for the manner in which you've handled this matter."

He had nothing to say about Celia Jensen. The partners found that easy to understand.

"I hope you'll be able to do something for Pickens," Rainbow told him. "He came through for us when things looked pretty tough, Mr. Conroy."

"I'll be going up to the job tomorrow. I'll have Mike move him up a little. You need a check. If you'll step out to the cashier's office, we can take care of that. Are you going to be in Denver for a day or two?"

"No, sir," Grumpy declared wryly. "We're pullin' out before somebody has the notion to put a pick and shovel in our hands. I whittled a couple years off my life on your Eureka job."

Conroy smiled. "Moran told me you were finding the going a little rough."

The partners found themselves in Cheyenne that evening and after a three-hour wait began the long trip across Wyoming.

"Could I interest you in a trip into the Solomons for deer this fall?" Rainbow asked, as they sat in the observation car.

"Not me," the little one said flatly. "You better talk to Dan Messenger. Mebbe you can persuade him to knock off for a week in the mistaken idea that a deer-hunt in that high country is just the thing to make a man fit and sassy. Personally, I'll take my fun a little easier. If the Bar 7 round-up is movin' toward home by the time I've caught up with my loafin', I may go out to the wagon for a day or two and do nothin' but exercise my jaw a little and leave it to someone else to do the sweatin'.."

CHAPTER 10

WHEN RIP AND GRUMPY ARRIVED in Black Forks the next morning, they found the hotel bus waiting at the depot. They got in with several traveling salesmen and rode up to the Bridger House. It was their custom whenever they wanted to linger in town for a few days before going out to Bar 7 to put up there.

After they had registered and refreshed themselves Rainbow suggested that they walk up to the court house and say hello to Judge Carver.

On the way up, they stopped half a dozen times to exchange greetings with old acquaintances. At the court house, they were disappointed to learn that the judge had gone out to the ranch.

"Let's drop around and see Rainsford," said Grumpy. "He always knows the news."

Buck saw them coming down the walk and came to the door to meet them.

"So you're back," he said. "I suppose you just got in."

"On the Limited," Rainbow told him. "She was running 'way late. We just heard we'd missed the judge."

"Yeh, he went out yesterday. How did you make out down in Colorado?"

"Dang near killed ourselves on that case," Grumpy complained. "We blew it wide open, but you shoulda seen us out there on the right-of-way swinging a pick."

"You seem to have plenty pepper left," Rainsford said, with a grin. "Suppose the two of you sit down. I don't suppose you've seen Messenger." Rip said no. "Dan's anxious to see you," Buck continued. "When you leave, I'll walk back to his office with you. Dan's got Johnnie Smiley workin' for him—cleanin' up the buildin' and givin' Mrs. Messenger a hand at the house."

"I bet Dan's anxious to see you," Grumpy declared, with

a caustic chuckle. "It's got somethin' to do with that wild horse you bought the Kid. It won't surprise me if they're gittin' ready to sue you."

Rainbow took it with a smile. "How did Johnnie make out with that big buckskin?"

"I don't know what to say," Buck drawled. "I ain't supposed to do any talkin'; the Kid asked me not to. But without lettin' the cat git too far out of the bag, I reckon I can tell you he did all right. Nothin' has ever meant as much to him as that horse, Rip. If they take him away from the Kid it's goin' to break his heart."

"Who's thinking of doing that?" Rainbow inquired, his tone indicating his immediate interest.

"Pike Kendrick. It's just a vague sort of a threat so far, but it's got the Kid scared stiff. We can talk it over with Dan and see what you make of it. I don't suppose you've heard that Steve Ellis was killed the other day."

"Killed?" Grumpy demanded. "You mean shot to death?"

Buck nodded. He told them about the slaying at the Tipstone stage station.

"The circumstances are suspicious but I haven't been able to dig up anythin' to warrant takin' Mundy into custody. The matter just rests there."

"Sounds like it was an unpremeditated killin', and that's always the hardest kind to unravel," Grumpy declared soberly. Rip and he had known Steve Ellis for years. It gave them a personal as well as professional interest in his death. "Three witnesses, but all prejudiced, I'd say."

"Two of them prejudiced and the other either intimidated or bribed, and I'm inclined to believe it's the former," said Rip. "They say Ike Cain always has a side of beef cooling out in his cellar. He doesn't have cows of his own, so I presume when he needs meat he just goes out and drops his loop where it'll do most good. I'm coupling that, Buck, with the fact that Mundy spends more time in the saddle than most foremen do; his riding takes him into every nook and cranny of Arrowhead."

"Your conclusion bein' that he caught Ike in an embarrassin' situation." Rainsford's eyes puckered thoughtfully. "I reckon I can believe that without stretchin' my imagination too much. Of course, to say that Mundy'd keep a thing like that under his hat on the chance that he might need Ike some day is just another way of sayin' he's a crook. I'm not ready to go that far; I know he's mean and doesn't give a damn for anyone but himself, but that doesn't necessarily make him a blackleg."

"By gravy, that's leanin' over backwards to be fair to a man!" Grumpy declared with characteristic vehemence. "I don't claim to know too much about Mundy but the little I got to hang my opinion on don't help him any with me. As I git it, he claims they was facin' each other when Ellis got his gun out of the leather. You couldn't make me believe that in a month of Sundays."

"What makes you so sure about it?" Buck questioned.

"Because he claims Ellis was drunk. You can't tell me Mundy stood there and let a drunken man draw on him. For my money, his story is a lie any way you look at it."

"That's only an opinion, Grump," Rainsford said, his tone unruffled. "I told you the circumstances were suspicious. I think Mundy's lying. But you see, you boys have got it on me; you can play your hunches; I've got to have some evidence before I can do anythin'."

"Ike Cain is your best bet, Buck," Rainbow spoke up. "He's often been in trouble with the law—nothing serious —but I imagine he knows his luck will run out on him and he'll go over the road for a stretch if you and Ashforth ever get a case against him that will stand up. I believe if you could convince him that you had dug up something— I don't mean anything connected with the shooting—you could break him down by offering to make a deal with him. I know he's as crooked as the day is long, but he's never going to make anyone any real trouble."

The sheriff shook his head. "I tried that, Rip. The old cuss wouldn't take the bait. If you boys want to take a day off, I'll appreciate it if you'll go up to Tipstone with me. Maybe you can get somethin' out of Ike."

Rainbow laughed. "That's putting us on the spot, Buck.

It's unlikely that our luck would be any better than yours. I think we better forget it for the time being."

"So do I," the little one agreed. "Let this thing simmer for a while, Buck. Later on we can show up at the Tipstone station. If Rip and me go alone it'll give us a free hand, and you won't be responsible for what we do. If we're goin' to have a talk with Messenger, we better be gittin' over there; it's almost dinner-time."

They caught Dan as he was leaving.

"We don't want to hold you up," Grumpy told him. "We can git together this afternoon just as well."

"No, we'll go up and sit down for a minute or two," said Messenger. "I want you to hear what I've got to say before you run into Johnnie. I suppose Buck has told you the boy is afraid they're going to take his horse away from him."

Rainbow nodded. "I can't understand it, Dan. It seems incredible that Kendrick would have any interest in an eight-dollar horse."

Messenger showed them into his office. The conversation turned almost immediately to what Kendrick had said on his visit to the flats.

"Tremaine was there at the time," Messenger told the partners. "I had a chance to speak to him the other day. He says Pike made it appear that he recognized the horse."

"Kendrick is wrong in his contention that unbranded livestock, runnin' wild, doesn't pass into the public domain," Grumpy asserted. "The courts have ruled on that a thousand times. If I find an unbranded cow roamin' my range and I take possession of it and slap my brand on the critter, it's mine."

"That's true," Dan agreed, "but this is a different matter. If you bring unbranded livestock into town and I buy it, the bill of sale I get from you gives me nominal title. But the law contends, Grumpy, that if a dispute arises over the ownership of the animals that the burden of proving legal title to them rests on me. If prima-facie evidence of their previous ownership is introduced, and I'm unable to contradict it, the court will order me to hand them over, and the only thing I can do is try to recover from you."

"This talk's getting beyond me," Rainbow said, with a puzzled frown. "I repeat what I said downstairs; what is there about an eight-dollar horse to interest Pike Kendrick?"

"You've got to put your cards on the table, Dan," Rainsford advised. "I know you don't want to spoil the surprise the Kid's been savin' for Rip, but it can't be helped."

"You're right," Messenger agreed. "When you see Johnnie, you don't have to let on that you know anything. The truth is, Pike's afraid that eight-dollar horse may win the stake race."

Rainbow and Grumpy brought their chairs down with a surprised bang.

"No!" the tall man exclaimed. "It passes belief, Dan!"

"It's a fact. Johnnie hasn't had any other idea in his mind from the moment he got his hands on the horse. He took him down on the flats, built a brush corral and proceeded to break him. I gave him a saddle. It wasn't long before he was working him out on the dirt road out to the old icehouse. He's had him shod."

"Good gravy!" Grumpy burst out. "That takes the cake! Is that big buckskin fast, Dan?"

Messenger shrugged. "I don't know. But he's big and strong enough to be fast, and he's got a good set of legs. I've never heard the boy express an opinion about it, but he calls him Champ, and he means it. Buck and I felt that he was reaching for the moon and that we ought to try to talk him out of any notion of racing the horse. He told me you'd bought Champ for him, Rip, and that he'd do whatever you said. You can guide yourself accordingly."

A smile softened the tall man's lean face.

"If the Kid's got an idea like that planted in his mind, it won't be easy to talk him out of it. The buckskin must have something if Kendrick is getting worried."

"He ain't the only one," Rainsford drawled. "Collamore offered the Kid fifty dollars the other day if he'd guarantee to stay away from the rodeo with Champ. Men who bet on horses scare awful easy. As far as I know, none of 'em has the slightest reason for thinkin' the Kid has the ghost of a show. I reckon it's only because he just looks mysterious and doesn't have anythin' to say when he's questioned about Champ that's got them sittin' on the edge of their seats. One of the boys in the court house told me he'd heard the horse was a sleeper we'd dug up and the Kid was only ridin' for us. That'll give you some idea of the nonsense that's goin' around."

"We can't stop folks from talkin', but between the four of us we ought to be able to see that the Kid gits a square deal," said Grumpy. "I figgered it was a mistake to hand that outlaw over to him; I didn't see what he was goin' to do with the horse, 'cept git hurt. To come home and find he's still in one piece and got the whole town by the ears kinda leave me flabbergasted. But if Johnnie can show me that the buckskin can travel with fast steppers like the Chief and Black Lightnin', I ain't goin' to sit back and see Pike Kendrick or anyone else do him out of his chance if I can help it."

Rainbow glanced across the desk at Messenger.

"What do you want us to do, Dan? Kendrick's talk may have been just a bluff. He hasn't made any move, has he?"

"I don't know for sure, Rip, but I think so. You remember Charlie Guthrie, of course. When Charlie died, his wife sold off what little livestock they had left and leased the range to Steve Ellis. She was never able to dispose of the brand and buildings. The other day, Pike bought her out for a song. The deed has just been recorded. Maybe it doesn't mean anything, but for the life of me I can't see why he'd want the brand for any legitimate reason. Charlie used to have some good horses. I'm just wondering if that explains anything. Pike is in a position now to put in a claim on any animal that may have broken away from the ranch."

"But Guthrie's dead. If Kendrick contends that Champ was Guthrie's horse, and not his, how is he going to prove it. He'll need witnesses and have to be able to identify the animal."

"I haven't the slightest idea how Kendrick is going to establish his case. I'm far from sure that he's even contemplating any legal action. But I was going to ask you to see if you could learn anything. I know if Champ was foaled on the Guthrie ranch he must have broken away when he was a yearling. It's possible that Mrs. Guthrie recalls the incident and will be a witness. That may be the very reason why Kendrick was tempted to buy her out. She's an old woman and she's been in hard straits for a long time. The prospect of a little unexpected cash would most likely quicken her imagination if not her memory."

Before Rainbow could answer, Grump said, "Sounds to me like you'd put yore finger on somethin'. It gives us two reasons for goin' up to Tipstone. I know if the old woman is mixed up in anythin' like this it's because somebody's pulled the wool over her eyes."

Rip nodded. "That would be my opinion. "You haven't said anything to Johnnie about this, I take it."

"No," Dan assured him. "It'll be time enough for that when we know what we're facing."

"I'm ready to do what I can," Rainbow announced. He glanced at Rainsford. "How about some horses, Buck? Can you fix us up?"

"Sure."

"All right, we'll pull away early tomorrow morning. If you haven't anything better to do, come over to the Bridger and have dinner with us; we'll let Dan run along home."

Rainsford accepted the invitation. They found Grat Collamore in the dining room. He stopped them as they passed his table. Relations between the partners and him had always been on a friendly level.

"I'm glad to see you back," he said. "You started something when you bought that horse for the Kid," he continued, with a dubious chuckle. "I suppose Buck's been giving you an earful."

"It was quite a surprise," was Rip's smiling answer. "I understand you're a little upset about it."

"No, slightly interested; that's all," Grat corrected. He buttered a biscuit carefully. "Being a prudent man, I try to walk around trouble when I see it shaping up ahead of me. I don't ask for a sure thing, whether it's a game of cards or a horse race. But a race is hard enough to figure no matter how much you know about the starters. Running in a wild horse on a man is like asking him to play with a loaded deck. The Kid should have grabbed my fifty dollars when he had the chance."

"Why did you withdraw yore offer?" Grumpy was quick with the question.

It took Collamore by surprise but without making any serious dent in his inscrutability. He picked up his knife and fork and then set them down again.

"The Kid will tell you I promised him he'd get a square deal from me. That still goes. It ain't going to help him a bit. I don't claim any virtues for myself, but I draw the line at handing the works to a boy. Maybe you can do something for him. I hope so, at least."

Rainbow thought he understood. His face whipped hard and flat.

"Is that as far as you can go, Grat?"

"It ought to be far enough for you, Rip," Collamore replied phlegmatically. "Pike means business. The funny part of it is that he's being taken for a sucker. There's more to this than doing the Kid out of his horse, but that ain't my business." With knife and fork in hand, he speared a piece of meat quickly and transferred it to his mouth.

His eyes remained locked with Rip's as the latter hung on, silently demanding a further explanation.

"All right!" Collamore growled. "I never heard any reason given why Joe Mundy was at the Tipstone station the day he shot Steve Ellis. Maybe he went up there just for a drink. But it's a long ride for a drink."

Rainbow's mouth relaxed. "Thanks Grat," he muttered, as he walked on with Grumpy and Rainsford.

"By Josephine, I can tell you now who Kendrick's witness is goin' to be!" the little one ground out, as they sat down. "That thievin', watery-eyed old reprobate Ike Cain is yore man!"

"No doubt of it," Rainsford grumbled. Rip leveled his gray eyes at him.

"Buck, if Mundy is rigging this business on Kendrick, you know what he's after. It ought to clear up any doubt in your mind as to what he is."

"It does!" Rainsford muttered grimly. "I've got him tagged correctly at last!"

CHAPTER 11

AFTER DINNER, RAINBOW AND GRUMPY stepped out on the hotel veranda with Rainsford and found the Kid standing on the sidewalk, waiting for them. He had been there all the while they were inside. His face lit up eagerly on catching sight of them.

"Rip!" he cried, rushing up. "Gee, I'm glad to see you and Grumpy! Mr. Messenger told me you'd got back. I been lookin' for you for a week."

The boy was so genuinely happy at seeing him that Rip was touched. He put his arm on the Kid's shoulder.

"Johnnie, you're looking fine! I was glad to hear you'd found a job in town. Dan must be treating you all right."

"We git along good, Rip. Mr. and Mrs. Messenger are fine people." The Kid gave Rainsford a long glance. "You didn't let nothin' slip about the horse, did you, Buck?"

"Say, what about that big buckskin?" Rainbow demanded, relieving the sheriff from answering the boy's question. "All I can get so far is that you've got a surprise for me. You don't mean to tell me you gentled him."

Johnnie grinned, and he was completely happy for the moment.

"When can you and Grumpy come down to see him?"

"We want to see him right away," the little one told

him. "We was goin' down now. Will you come along, Buck?"

"No, I can't, Grump. I'll be busy most of the afternoon. But you boys go along with Johnnie. I'll see you later on."

The Kid stretched his legs and kept in step with the tall man as they walked down the street. He had been sorely beset for days, but the return of the partners, especially of Rainbow, gave him a feeling of security and confidence that neither Buck nor Messenger had been able to inspire. Just to walk down the main street of Black Forks with Rip and Grumpy was a tonic in itself and he made the most of this opportunity to let people see that these men were his friends. Acquaintances with whom he would ordinarily have exchanged a word got only a nod.

A sixteen-horse freighting outfit was pulling away from Rinehart's warehouse as they passed.

"Gittin' a late start," Grumpy remarked. "It'll be after midnight before they reach the Tipstone station."

The reference to Tipstone had a sobering effect on the Kid.

"Reckon you've been told what happened to Steve Ellis," he said.

"Yes," Rip acknowledged, "Buck told us. We were sorry to hear it."

After a momentary hesitation the boy said, "What do you fellas make of it?"

"We haven't had time to think about it." Rainbow's evasiveness was intentional. "I was glad to hear that Dan and Tremaine had advised you as they did. Have you seen any more of Mundy?"

"No. I guess he ain't been in lately. I saw Kendrick."

"Yeh?" Rip said, giving the boy a chance to say more.

"He was after me to ride Black Lightnin'. He found out that I meant it when I said no." The Kid looked up and his young face was pinched with anxiety suddenly. "Rip, can he take my horse away from me? He as good as threatened to do it. I spoke to Mr. Messenger about it."

"What did Dan tell you?" Grumpy put in.

"That if anythin' came up, he'd look out for my interests."

"That's a good answer, Johnnie," said Rainbow. "Pike Kendrick is inclined to be hot-headed. I wouldn't lose any sleep over it. We'll be around. If anybody tries to do you dirt, we'll have somethin' to say about it. Here's the path. It's been a long time since I was down on the flats. Looks like someone had been cutting some willows."

"That was me," the boy told him. "I made a brush corral for Champ. Couldn't keep him on a picket rope all the time."

"You named him Champ, eh?" Rip inquired innocently.

"You like it, Rip?"

"It's a fine name for a horse. Is he living up to it, Johnnie?"

"I wouldn't trade him for any horse I ever saw," was the Kid's stoutly loyal response. "He'll nicker as soon as he hears me comin'. I reckon he thinks as much of me as I do of him. The two of us shore hit it off, Rip. He ain't wild no more. I been runnin' him some."

"Johnnie, do you mean it?" Rainbow's surprise was so well simulated the boy did not question it.

"You'll be tellin' us you got a race horse next," Grumpy put in for good measure.

Johnnie's grin returned. "I shore wouldn't try to fool you fellas. Grat Collamore and some others have been doin' some talkin' and kinda snoopin' around. But they ain't got nothin' out of me; I just kept on sawin' wood, waitin' for you to git back. I figgered if I had him all ready you'd be proud of him, too."

This glimpse into what was in the boy's heart tightened Rip's mouth and he silently vowed to lay aside his own plans for the present and devote all his time and energy to checkmating Pike Kendrick and his foreman.

Champ whinnied. It brought Mr. Smiley to the cabin door, for it had become a signal to him that the boy was in sight. Johnnie had bought his father a pair of dark glasses. He had seen them displayed on a card in Rinehart's, priced at twenty-five cents. Cheap as they were, Mr.

Smiley claimed they helped his eyes, and he wore them incessantly.

"Hi yuh, Wash!" Grumpy called to him.

Though the voice sounded familiar, Mr. Smiley had difficulty in recognizing the little man. When he did, a smile wreathed his pink, rather childish face.

"By gum, it's the little runt!" he exclaimed. "That Rainbow you got with you?"

"Yep, it's the two of us."

They reached the cabin door a few moments later and Mr. Smiley shook hands with them.

"Come in and take a load off yore feet," he urged. "Johnnie and me has been talkin' about you considerable, wonderin' jest when you'd git home. It's shore comfortin' to know yo're around."

"We want to see the horse first, Mr. Smiley," Rip told him. "We'll stop in before we leave."

"All right," the old man sputtered. "Reckon the hoss is the big item." His attention turned to Johnnie. "You git my lemon drops?"

"Pappy, there ain't a lemon drop in town nowheres. They had somethin' new in Rudy's Smoke Shop, called cream delights, two for a penny. Rudy said they was real tasty. He had me try one, and I liked it fine."

He pulled out a small paper bag and handed it to his father. Mr. Smiley reached inside and squashed one of the cream delights.

"Soft candy," he complained, licking his fingers. "Soft candy is all right for them that likes it, but you put it in yore mouth and it's gone before you can say Jack Robinson. That's one thing about lemon drops I like; they're lastin'."

Rainbow thought the old man looked more feeble than when he had seen him last. On the way to the corral, however, he said, "Your father seems to be about as usual."

"I don't know," the Kid answered weightily. "Gittin' so he has awful tantrums when he puts somethin' down and can't find it. When I came home yesterday afternoon, he was crawlin' around on the cabin floor, lookin' for his pipe. It was on the table all the time. His eyes is worse than he figgers, I reckon. But I'm savin' up fast as I can. I'll git him to one of those big eye doctors before long."

Rip nodded and stole a glance at Grump. The latter said, "If things pan out all right there won't be no trouble about that."

Champ eyed the partners nervously, but Johnnie spoke to him and finally induced him to come up to the gate.

Rainbow and Grumpy were honestly amazed.

"By grab, he looks fit as a fiddle!" the little man declared enthusiastically. "His coat's shinin' and he looks hard. You must have been grainin' him for some time."

"Yeh." The Kid was waiting for Rainbow to express his opinion. "Ain't you got nothin' to say, Rip?"

"Johnnie, I hardly know what to say. He's a beauty. It doesn't seem possible this is the same horse I saw in the shipping pens. Mustang said he was wild, and he sure was. I never admitted it to Grumpy, but after we left for Denver I had some misgivings about buying this fellow for you. How long have you had the shoes on him?"

The Kid understood what was behind the question.

"You don't have to worry about his hoofs, Rip. The shoes are just as tight as they was the minute Hoeffler got through puttin' 'em on. Be almost a week today. But I got even better news for you. I really let him out this mornin' about daylight. Man, can he pack the mail! I got him warmed up nice before I give him the word. I didn't have no measured distance nor any way of holdin' a watch on him, but he was movin'. Black Lightnin' never showed me anythin' like that."

"Wal, we can step off three-eighths of a mile without no trouble," Grump chirped. "Ed Bosch has always got a stop watch in his jewelry store. I'll borrow one off him."

The Kid's spirits soared; he had been looking forward to this moment for a long time.

"We'll git everythin' attended to this afternoon and be ready for the trial in the mornin'," he said happily. "We don't want no snoopers hangin' around. You won't mind gittin' out of bed early, will you?"

Rainbow said no. He did not mention the fact that they were leaving for Tipstone at an early hour. After spending a few minutes at the cabin, they crossed the creek and went out towards the icehouse and carefully stepped off a stretch of three furlongs, the distance at which the stake race was run.

The Kid was sorry the work was finished so quickly, for he would have liked to have hung on to Rip and Grumpy for the rest of the afternoon. In the hope of getting them back to the corral for at least another few minutes, he said guilelessly, "I guess Champ's safe enough on the flats. Worries me some times, though. When I'm up-town doin' my job, Pappy's all alone. If he's workin' on a basket, he don't pay attention to anythin' goin' on outside. The corral's purty far from the cabin, don't you think?"

Rainbow said no. He was completely taken in.

"It's nicely placed, Johnnie. Makes it easy for you to fetch water from the creek. You don't have to worry about Champ being safe."

"I found a couple of cigarette butts on the path to the crick the other day. Someone had been around. You don't think they'd try to steal Champ or do somethin' to him? I could move the corral."

"You leave it where it is," Rip told him. "And forget about Pike Kendrick stealing your horse or trying to injure it. That's foolish. If he makes a move it'll be some legal skullduggery. He wants Black Lightning to win, and he'll go a long way to make sure of it. But you know he isn't a scoundrel. After all, you've got some friends on Arrowhead—one in particular."

"Resa?"

"Certainly! Pike knows he doesn't dare to do anything too raw or he'll be in trouble with her. We've got a few things to do, Johnnie. We'll get back to town. I—brought you back a little something from Denver. If you want to come down to the hotel after supper, I'll give it to you."

"Gosh, I didn't expect you to bring me nothin', Rip,"

the Kid said rather tremulously. "I'll be out in front of the Bridger about seven o'clock."

The partners saw him cross the creek as they followed the old road into town.

"He was hangin' on to you purty hard," Grumpy declared sympathetically. "Kinda lonesome for him down here with just old Wash around. I don't know why it is, but he gits under my hide, somehow. . . . I didn't know you bought anythin' for him in Denver."

"I didn't," Rainbow confessed. "I never thought of it. I'm going into Bosch's and buy him a time-piece. I'll swear Ed to keep my secret if Johnnie comes in some time to have it repaired. I don't think we'd better say anything to Ed about a stop watch. He'd surmise why we wanted it."

"I guess that's right," the little one acknowledged. "He does a lot of bettin' on the races. But where we goin' to git it?"

"I'll try at the school. I've seen Tom Lowry using one at the games. I'll walk up there right now."

His errand was successful. Later in the afternoon, he found a watch for Johnnie that suited him. Bosch laughed over his request never to mention that it had been purchased in his store.

"Rip, there's a dozen women in this town wearing bracelets and the like that are supposed to have come all the way from Kansas City to San Francisco. I'd have a lot of husbands in hot water if I started talking. I won't say anything to the Kid; you can depend on it. By the way, what do you know about that buckskin horse he's got down there on the flats?"

"I don't know a thing that would interest a betting man, Ed." Rip's eyes were as empty as an Indian's and a faint grin touched the corners of his mouth. "I imagine that's what you meant. If you'll put this in a chamois bag, I'll take it that way; you needn't wrap it up."

The Kid was on hand at the stroke of seven, his face freshly scrubbed. Rainbow called him up on the veranda and gave him the watch. "How does it strike you?" he asked, as Johnnie stood there speechless. "There wasn't time to have your name engraved on it."

The boy's lip quivered and he lowered his head to hide his emotion. "I—I don't know why you did anythin' like this, Rip," he got out chokingly. "It's the finest thing I ever owned—next to Champ."

"Sit down," Grumpy told him, his tone as gruff as usual. In the shadows, however, his flinty face had lost his grimness for the moment. "Rip figgered a watch was just about what you needed. You ought to have a chain to go with it. I got an extry one in my trunk at the ranch. I'll bring it to you next time."

The boy was further embarrassed. He regarded the little man with a deep intentness for a moment, his eyes large in his thin face.

"Do you think you ought to do that, Grumpy?" he asked tensely. "I'd admire to have a watch chain that belonged to you, but—"

"That's all settled," Grumpy growled, busying himself with his pipe. "I told Rip not to buy a chain, that I'd take care of that end."

It satisfied the Kid. Rainbow put him further at ease by turning the conversation to other things. He suspected the boy was anxious to show the watch to his father, and when he saw Rainsford coming, he said, "We'll see you in the morning, Johnnie. We'll be down early. The Messengers have invited us up to the house for the evening."

After proudly exhibiting the gift to Buck, the boy hurried off for home. Rainsford's glance followed him for a moment or two.

"Takes so little to make a boy happy," he mused.

The partners were in bed before midnight. Four o'clock came quickly. By the time they got into range clothes and stepped out of the hotel, dawn was breaking. Early as it was, Johnny was already astir, and when they reached the flats, he had Champ saddled.

Mr. Smiley popped out of the cabin and insisted on witnessing the trial. He almost fell in the creek before they got him across.

"This road ain't as fast as the track," the Kid reminded them. "You got to allow a second or two for that even at three furlongs."

"We'll take that into consideration," Rainbow told him. "I'll go down to the finish line and hold the watch. Grump will start you."

The little one had cut off a willow limb. He trimmed it with his knife and affixed a handkerchief.

"When I yell go, I'll drop the flag; keep yore eyes on me, Rip."

"Say, that leaves me out of it," Mr. Smiley protested. "Let me hold the flag."

Grumpy glared at him fiercely. "Wash, you git back in the brush and keep quiet. I'll paddle you if you do anythin' to distract the horse."

Johnnie had swung up into the saddle.

"Grumpy's right, Pappy," he said. "You keep back. I'll jog Champ up the road a bit and loosen him up a little."

The big horse seemed to realize the meaning of these preparations. He was so eager to run that the boy had difficulty holding him in.

The sun was up by the time he turned and started moving back toward Grumpy. The stake race was run from a standing start. With his boot heel, the little one had drawn a line across the road.

"Walk him up to it," he called to the Kid. "I'll give you time enough to git set before I yell go."

Champ was getting nervous, but Johnnie brought him up to the line.

"Hold him now!" Grumpy warned. "Git ready! Go!"

Champ broke away with a rush. The Kid flattened out on the stallion's neck and felt him respond to the pressure of his knees.

Grumpy's eyes were torn wide with amazement as he saw the big horse streaking down the road, the rhythmic beating of his flying hoofs ringing out on the morning air.

With every stride the buckskin's legs seemed to flash out at an increased tempo. In a matter of seconds, he flashed past Rainbow.

Mr. Smiley scampered out of the brush, garrulous and excited. Grumpy waved him out of the way and ran down the road to learn the time.

Johnnie had to take Champ almost to the icehouse before he could pull him down. He jogged back to where the partners stood, waiting.

"How good was it?" he jerked out breathlessly, encouraged by their obvious excitement.

"I clocked you in thirty-nine seconds flat." Rip did not try to conceal his elation. "That's better than good, Johnnie! The three furlong record for hot bloods is only thirty-three seconds."

"Three-eighths of a mile is just a breeze for him!" Grumpy declared. "He's hardly warmed up! What did you do on Black Lightnin', Johnnie?"

"Forty-one and two-fifths, they said. But he's done better'n forty-one." He patted Champ affectionately. "I got to keep you movin'; I don't want you to git stiff. . . . I don't put a blanket on him, Rip, till I git back across the creek. I walk him good, then." He had a question to ask, and because so much depended on the answer, he put it hesitantly. . . . "Do you figger he's good enough to put in the race?"

"He's good enough to win it, Johnnie," Rainbow replied. "I'm proud of both of you."

The Kid's cup of happiness overflowed.

"Gosh, I reckon that makes everythin' all right." He drew in a deep breath of relief. "I'll meet you at the corral."

Rainbow was compelled to tell him they had some business up north and were leaving Black Forks as soon as they could finish breakfast.

"But we'll be back tomorrow or sooner. You just tend to your knitting; things will work out all right."

The Kid was disappointed, but he said, "Shore! I'll be lookin' for you when you git back. I don't want to do no braggin', but Champ won't let you down. You can depend on that."

He rode away.

"And we won't let you down," Rainbow muttered soberly. "This is one case I don't propose to lose!"

"Them's my sentiments exactly!" Grumpy growled. "If they take the horse away from the Kid it'll be over my dead body and no way else!"

CHAPTER 12

THE AIR WAS SO CLEAR this late September morning that three hours of riding seemed to bring the blue-brown swell of the Solomons no nearer. Flung out in front of the main bulwark of the mountains like a protecting barrier reef were high hills. Beyond those hills lay Tipstone Valley.

This was familiar country to Rainbow and Grumpy. The road was the main one north and would have taken them to Bar 7 had they desired. They pulled up, however, when they reached the forks where it branched off to the valley, and rested their horses.

"The country looks good," the little one observed. It was the first time he had spoken in an hour. "It's been a better than average year for everybody." The buffalo grass was brown already, but it would lose none of its nutritive value until it dropped its seeds in the spring. Cattle were grazing in the distance. This was Double Diamond range. "Purcell's stuff looks fine. He's evidently goin' to have Tremaine work down this way last. I never could see any reason for doin' it otherwise. But a man gits set in his ways and it's hard to change him."

Rip nodded and let it pass without comment.

"It must be tough for Stark to ride over to Arrowhead to see Resa and run into Mundy," he mused. "Stark and Ellis were pretty close. He's level-headed, but there'll be trouble there some day."

"Only a question of time," Grumpy agreed. "If we're goin' to do anything about Mundy, we don't want to be too long."

It was their intention on reaching Tipstone to ride across the valley and learn what they could from Mrs. Guthrie before going near the station. They felt if they could get the old woman to talk they would be able to decide for themselves if Messenger's surmise was correct.

"I suppose we'll find her packin' up," said Grumpy. "She's got a sister livin' in town. Chances are Hattie will go in and stay with her. Unless she's bein' completely duped, she's been posted as to her story. What line are we goin' to take with her?"

"We can pretend we don't know she's sold out and that we're interested in buying the place. That'll give us an opening."

They crossed the valley several miles below the station and rode into the yard at the Guthrie place at noon. They saw evidence that the old woman was packing her belongings. Mrs. Guthrie was at the kitchen door by the time they got down. She knew who they were.

"What are you doin', Hattie, cleanin' house?" Grumpy inquired banteringly.

"No, I ain't, Mr. Gibbs; I'm packing. I've sold."

"What?" The little man's tone was sharp with disappointment. "That's too bad! When we heard Steve Ellis was dead and wouldn't be leasin' yore range no longer, we figgered we'd like to buy and add it to the acreage we've been puttin' together. We rode over to make you an offer."

"Wal, you gentlemen are too late. I've sold to Pike Kendrick. It's a pity, ain't it, that after settin' here, wantin' to sell for nigh on three years, that I should git two offers in one week. . . . I'd ask you in, but everythin's so upset. I'm expectin' a wagon to take my goods into Black Forks this afternoon."

Rainbow sat down on the edge of the water trough. "We won't bother you, Mrs. Guthrie. How did Mr. Kendrick happen to become interested in buying the place?"

"Wal, I don't rightly know." The old woman tucked her

scraggly hair into a tight knot. "Mr. Mundy, his foreman, came by one day recently and stopped in fer a minit.
He said Arrowhead might take everything off my hands at
a price. That range Steve was leasin' is good summer range,
you know. I didn't think it was more'n talk, but next I
knew, Mr. Kendrick rides over and we came to terms."

The partners exchanged a shrewd glance. To learn that
Mundy had had a part in arranging the sale went a long
way toward confirming the tip Grat Collamore had given
them.

"The price I took was a shame," Mrs. Guthrie continued. "Charlie and me scraped and slaved so long."

Grumpy primed the pump and helped himself to a drink
as she rattled on about her departed husband.

"Hattie, before Mundy said anythin' about gittin' Kendrick interested, was he inquirin' about a buckskin horse
that strayed away from the ranch?"

"He said he'd heard that Charlie lost a fine buckskin
yearlin'."

"He jogged yore memory about it a little, I reckon."

"Laws, he didn't have to! Charlie never got over losin'
that yearlin'. It happened the spring before Mr. Guthrie
passed away."

The old woman was beginning to grow suspicious of
their questions, but the partners were convinced that she
knew little or nothing about what was afoot.

"Charlie's been dead three years," said Rainbow. "That
would make the horse about four years old. That's going
back quite a spell. Who was working for you at that time,
Mrs. Guthrie?"

"Steve claimed he was workin' for us," she declared,
with a tart laugh. "He was allus more interested in flyin'
off to some dance or swappin' yarns down at the station
than in workin'."

Rainbow flashed a glance at Grumpy. The little one
nodded. Both had been quick to grasp that the old woman's
story was now open to contradiction.

"Yore memory's playin' tricks on you, Hattie," Grumpy
chided. "You know as well as I do that Steve Ellis was

workin' for Double Diamond for a year before he leased yore range. That would make it five years ago, not four, that the horse busted away from you."

Mrs. Guthrie was immediately confused.

"You git a body all tangled up with yore questions," she protested. "Mebbe it was five years ago, mebbe four. I don't see no point in talkin' about it nohow. I'd like to stand here and visit with you some more, but I got so much left to do, you got to excuse me."

"We won't waste any more of your time, Mrs. Guthrie," Rip told her, getting to his feet. "I'm sorry we were too late to make you an offer."

He and the little one swung up in the saddle.

"See you again, Hattie," the latter called back as they rode away.

They had learned enough to erase any doubt that Pike Kendrick was going to attempt to claim Champ. On the other hand, they were equally positive that they could entangle Hattie Guthrie in her story.

"She'll let Kendrick know we paid her a visit," Grumpy predicted. "He'll be smart enough to see she can't be much help to him."

"No doubt," Rainbow agreed. "According to her time table, Champ would be five years old or better. He may be four, but not a day more. That in itself would knock the bottom out of Kendrick's contention. I imagine he'll coach her to be vague about the time and be satisfied to have her testify that Charlie had a buckskin yearling that got away."

"If there's any hearin', we'll be present and have somethin' to say, Rip. I can understand exactly what Collamore meant when he said Pike was bein' taken for a sucker. Mundy rigged up this deal and then sold it to him. I can see just how it was worked; Ike Cain was plumb in the middle of it. He'd have heard from old Charlie about him losin' a horse. That's what sent Mundy up to see the old woman. What he found out from her left him nothin' to do but git Cain primed to come forward and identify the Kid's horse as the missin' animal. That's what's between that pair. When Mundy went to Pike with that setup, the old man couldn't stay away from it."

Rainbow had no fault to find with the little man's argument. He rode along without saying anything for several minutes.

"What's on yore mind?" Grumpy growled.

"I was just thinking how necessary it was to have Steve Ellis out of the way. A word from him would have knocked this business into a cocked hat."

Grumpy turned in his saddle and regarded the tall man with narrowed eyes.

"Mundy was well heeled that day," Rip added. "He had Pasco and Lesant with him. They've been the lone wolves of the Arrowhead crew ever since he brought them down from Windy River. A foreman doesn't usually take two men away from their work just to have company when he goes riding."

Grumpy rocked with the inference Rip had drawn and the lines in his face deepened.

"That could be the answer we're lookin' for! Mundy could have had 'em along to make shore his play wasn't goin' to miss. Cain will know why we're showin' up. He'll be cagey with us."

Rainbow nodded. "We'll get something out of him—one way or another."

Though the station at Tipstone was still referred to as a stage station, it had not seen a stage in years; the freighting outfits that plied between Black Forks and the mining camps on the western slope of the Solomon Mountains put up there over night and provided Cain with his chief source of revenue. The Government maintained a post office at Tipstone, but it paid him only a few dollars a year, and he had to depend on his bar and the freighters for a living. He was seated outside in a chair, sound‑asleep, when the partners rode up.

Ike slowly shook himself awake and blinked his rheumy eyes. When he recognized his visitors, he jerked wide awake in a hurry. Rip and Grumpy had last seen him a year ago, seated in the same spot and in the same chair. If he had changed at all it was only to become a little dirtier, his pants a little baggier at the knees. The days were long, here at Tipstone, with very little to break the monotony, and through the years old Ike had become the living counterpart of the shabby station, his drooping mustache and beaten, hang-dog look a perfect reflection of the sagging barns and woebegone windows, the holes in the broken panes either stuffed with rags or boarded up if rags didn't suffice to keep out dust or cold, depending on the season.

"Ain't seen you fellas in a long time," he said without enthusiasm. He got to his feet, tall and stringy, regarding them the while with a crafty if obscure interest. Behind him, the saloon door stood wide open. He turned in and went behind the bar. The partners stepped in after him and Rip spun a silver dollar on the mahogany.

"I got some cold beer and rye; that's all." Ike didn't expect this visit to be pleasant, and his tone indicated as much.

"Beer," Grumpy told him. Rip said the same.

"Reckon yo're goin' to ask questions about Steve." Ike pulled the caps off the bottles. "I told Rainsford all I know."

"We figgered we'd like to git it first-hand; we knew Steve." Grumpy raised his glass and smacked his lips. "This beer *is* cold. You musta had it buried in the spring."

Cain nodded. "Didn't fetch it up but a few minutes ago. Mundy had to shoot in self-defense. It was one or t'other of 'em. I miss Steve. I could allus depend on him to show up onct a week fer his mail and a drink or two."

"Ike, where was he standing when Mundy dropped him?" Rip had located the hole in the ceil..g from which the sheriff had removed the slug from Ellis' gun.

"Right thar in the door. He was goin' out to his hoss. I don't know why he didn't keep on goin'."

"Where was Mundy standing?"

"Jest about whar yuh are."

"And Lesant and Pasco?"

"They was leanin' on the bar, about hyar." Ike indicated the spot. "I was right whar I am now, not more'n an inch or two one way or t'other."

Rainbow had Grump stand where Cain said Mundy had been. He walked to the door, himself.

"Let's act this out and get it straight," he said. "This is the way Mundy, Steve and you were standing. Is that right?"

"That's correct," Ike assured him.

"You're positive?"

"Absolutely!"

Grumpy held his tongue, wondering what Rip was trying to prove. He saw him whip up his gun suddenly and level it at him. Behind the bar, Cain started to duck.

Rip grinned. "You're a little nervous, Ike. Did you duck down behind the bar like that when Ellis flashed his gun? You knew he was mad and that he meant business when he drew. That's what you told Rainsford."

Ike's Adam's apple slid up and down in his throat with a convulsive jerk. He saw the pitfall ahead of him.

"I know I did," he acknowledged uneasily. "But I held my ground."

"You were right in the line of fire, but you stayed put; yet just now you were ready to drop." Rip laughed accusingly. "That was a bad slip you made, Ike."

Cain started to make a denial. Grumpy cut him short.

"You lyin' old reprobate, yo're caught with yore pants down! If that shootin' was run off as you claim, you'd have hit the floor the second Ellis reached for his gun! Yo're either lyin' about it or you didn't see what happened at all! What's Mundy got on you that yo're eatin' out of his basket this way?"

"He ain't got nuthin' on me!" Ike protested vehemently. "I'm tellin' it the way I saw it!"

"Let's see if you are," Rainbow said thinly. "I'll take your word that you were standing there and saw Ellis draw. Now you watch me." He returned his gun to the holster. "You saw Ellis fire, you say. I'm going to draw now. When my hand starts up, you stop me when I reach the position he was in when he shot."

Rainbow made a leisurely draw. His hand went up and up, Cain sucked in his breath with a throaty rasp. No other sound came from him. A harried look tugged at his watery eyes.

"What's the matter? Was I too fast for you?" Rainbow regarded him with chilling intentness. "We'll try it again; and you sing out or get ready to crawl."

Rip's hand moved slower this time.

"About thar," Ike growled.

The gun was more than shoulder high. It was incredible to the partners that any man, even a tipsy one, who had handled a Colt all his life, would have been in that position. But Rip squeezed the trigger. The bullet thudded into the wall within a few inches of the ceiling.

The shot filled the barroom with a rumbling thunder. It rolled through the open door and died away. No one moved. Cain's ragged mustache dropped forlornly. Though he was ignorant, he knew his rights: the partners were detectives, but they were not the law. Officially, they had no authority to question and push him around like this. He exacted little comfort from the knowledge, for he realized that if he tried to defy them he would be inviting more trouble.

"Come out from behind the bar and walk over here," Rainbow ordered. "I want you to explain something to me."

Ike shuffled across the room.

"I don't know what yo're up to," he whined, "but if yo're goin' to do any more shootin', don't bust the mirror fer me."

"I won't break your mirror," Rip assured him. "You saw where my bullet landed. If Ellis had his gun in the same position I did, tell me how his slug ploughed into the ceiling."

Cain wiped his mouth with the back of his hand and

contemplated the bullet hole in the planks above with squinting eyes.

"I don't know as I can explain it," he muttered, trying to crawl out of the trap he was in. "Mebbe Steve had his gun higher than I figgered."

"He would have had to have it over his head!" Rainbow rapped. "Like this!"

He put a bullet into the ceiling within several inches of the hole.

"There's only one explanation of it!" Grumpy ground out. He detached himself from the bar. "Mebbe I can jog yore memory a little, Ike! Ellis had his gun up like that because he'd been hit and was droppin' to the floor! In tryin' to save himself from goin' down, he tightened his grip on the gun and it went off! Don't tell me he was shootin' at Mundy, you moth-eaten old liar!"

His manner was so threatening that Cain backed off a step.

"Call me a liar as much as yuh please, but don't you crowd me too far, Gibbs!" he got out shrilly. "Pasco and Lesant saw it the same way I did. Yore guessin' at what happened don't make it so."

"You'll find we're doing something more than guessing," Rainbow advised. "This case is a long way from being closed. I wonder if you know what you're letting yourself in for in suppressing evidence? If it turns out to be murder, you'll be an accessory after the fact and the law will hold you as responsible as the actual killer."

"I ain't serpressin' nuthin'!" Ike retorted with growing truculence. Desperation was giving him his second wind. "I'll be right hyar whenever the sheriff wants me. And I kin tell yuh sunthin': when you go around accusin' an innocent man, yo're leavin' yoreselves liable. Reckon Joe Mundy will know what to do about it!"

"We'll be glad to have him take exception to anything we've said," the tall man informed him. "Perhaps he'll be willing to explain what he was doing here that afternoon. You wouldn't know, would you?"

"I ain't in the habit of askin' people thar business when they drop in," was Cain's curt answer.

"It's a thirty-mile ride over here from Arrowhead," Rip remarked. "That's a considerable distance. If a man didn't have some legitimate business at the end of it, a jury might feel it called for an explanation."

"Yeh, seein' that he was droppin' in reg'lar," the little one threw in. "Or was that the only time he was here, Ike?"

Cain was tempted to say yes, but he was too smart to trap himself a second time.

"Mundy never came over this-a-way much. Reckon he was up here onct before."

"Was that the time he went up to see Mrs. Guthrie?" Rip asked quickly.

"Reckon it wuz," Ike answered, deciding that a little truthfulness now might help. "He went up to talk to her about a hoss Charlie lost some years back." It was unexpected enough to startle the partners. Cain enjoyed the surprise.

"I suppose you told him about Guthrie's buckskin," Rainbow suggested.

"I shore did! I 'membered the hoss wal. Best colt Charlie ever owned." The proprietor of the Tipstone station grew bold enough to laugh in their faces. "Yuh fellas ain't kiddin' me; I know all about that hoss the Kid's got down on the flats outside of Black Forks. I was in town last week and managed to git a good look at the hoss. I recognized him right off."

"You dirty crook!" Grumpy rapped. "I oughta pull the hide off you! There's a lot of buckskin stallions in this country! The idea of you claimin' you can recognize a horse you ain't see in years!"

"I'm used to bein' abused," Ike cackled. "I ain't got nuthin' ag'in the Kid, but he won't have that hoss long. There's a mark on him that I'm going by. Sunthin' yuh fellas didn't notice, I reckon."

"What kind of a mark?" Rainbow whipped out, his face

hard and flat. Cain knew he had the upper hand now, and he just stood there and grinned.

"I'll be tellin' that to the jedge, if yuh don't mind, Ripley."

The partners did not linger long after that. They were in a sober mood as they headed for town.

"Reckon that explains the cigarette butts the Kid found," Grumpy growled savagely. "Cain's seen some little peculiarity on Champ that he'll swear Guthrie's horse had. If they can git old Hattie to do just enough lyin' to back that up, they'll come mighty close to takin' the horse away from Johnnie."

"I know it," Rainbow muttered grimly. "I'm afraid it's coming too quickly for us to stop it."

"There's one thing we can do, Rip. We can hide Champ."

The tall man shook his head.

"We'd be in contempt. The judge would never forgive us."

"Wal, you keep out of it, then," the little one returned, his hard-bitten face set and determined. "I'll handle it. If I have to do anythin', I won't wait for a court order to be issued."

CHAPTER 13

IT WAS AFTER TEN O'CLOCK when the partners reached town. They rode to Rainsford's barn and stabled the broncs. There was a light in the sheriff's office. They walked that way and found Toby Ferris, the deputy sheriff, on duty.

"I suppose Buck's gone home for the night, Toby," Rainbow said.

"No, he went down the street about ten minutes ago to get a snack, Rip. I think you'll catch him in the Crescent Lunch. If he ain't there, try the barbecue."

They found the sheriff perched on a stool in the lunch room. There were four or five other customers.

"Well?" Buck inquired guardedly.

"We did all right," Rip replied. "Haven't had any supper. We'll sit down with you, and go up to the hotel afterwards."

Rainsford nodded. "That'll be better, I reckon. You needn't hurry. You must be hungry."

Grumpy asked for a double order of ham and eggs and fried potatoes.

"And give me some coffee while I'm waitin'," he told the man behind the counter.

Buck laughed. "I'll say one-half of the combination is hungry."

"That goes for both of us," Rainbow remarked, with a grin. "I forgot to mention that he missed dinner, too."

When they finally got to the Bridger, Rip got the key at the desk and led the way upstairs to the connecting rooms Grumpy and he were occupying. The little one sat down and pulled off his boots immediately.

"I'm in for the night," he observed, tossing his coat on the bed and getting out his pipe and tobacco. "We saw Cain and Hattie Guthrie, Buck, and managed to git quite an earful. But I don't know what Rip means by sayin' we did all right. It looks purty bad for the Kid."

He couldn't find a chair that suited him, so he went into his room and dragged out a rocker. He was in time to catch the end of a question Rainsford had addressed to Rainbow.

"It's exactly what Dan said," Rip answered. "Kendrick is going to try to prove that Champ belonged to Charlie Guthrie. Mundy's got the old lady all primed to make a statement. Ike Cain is going to identify the horse. It's a faked up story from start to finish. But as Grump says, it looks like they'll get away with it. If we had even a little evidence on our side, it would be different."

They gave him a detailed account of their talk with Mrs. Guthrie, as well as their conclusions about it. From that, they went on to what Ike had had to say regarding the horse.

"Of course that dirty skunk is lyin'!" Buck exclaimed disgustedly. "I can't believe Pike Kendrick would swallow a yarn like that unless he wanted to; he knows Ike Cain is a worthless renegade. I doubt that the judge will order the Kid to hand Champ over on his word. Did you get anythin' out of Cain about Ellis?"

Grumpy said, "We got plenty, Buck. Rip had him hangin' on the ropes. We came away from Tipstone convinced that Steve was cut down without havin' a chance for his life. He was leavin' when somebody called to him, and when he turned, he got it."

"There can't be any question about it," Rainbow seconded. "We proved to our satisfaction that Steve Ellis didn't fire the first shot. We're sure he'd had a slug pumped into him before he got his gun out of the holster."

"Suppose you boys start at the beginnin' and let me draw my own conclusions," Rainsford advised.

The partners obliged with a graphic story of what had taken place at the Tipstone station that afternoon. It had the sheriff shaking his head long before they were finished. At the end, he sat there without saying anything for a minute.

"Do you see it the way we do?" Rainbow asked.

"Yes; I don't see how it would be possible to read anythin' else into it," Rainsford responded soberly. "I wouldn't say you'd busted things wide open, but you've certainly got your foot in the door. I couldn't have gone up there and did anythin' like that—makin' my points with a loaded gun. There would have been a howl from the voters that I was exceedin' my authority. What do you expect Mundy to do about it? You've accused him of murder in no uncertain way."

"I don't expect him to do anything, Buck," the tall man replied. "Legally, I mean. We're convinced he's guilty. If we're right, he won't rush into court and give us a chance to put him under oath and start firing questions. If we accomplished nothing else, we made Cain change his story. And that can be damaging. All four of them told you the same tale, didn't they?"

"Word for word. They had plenty time to git their heads together before I got there that night. What's your point?"

"That all four of them couldn't have been mistaken. With Cain being compelled to change his story, it would be apparent to a jury that the statement they made to you couldn't have been true."

"I could bring Lesant and Pasco in and grill them," the sheriff offered.

Rip said, "Don't waste your time on them, Buck. Ike Cain is the key to this case. Mundy had something on him to whip him into line in the beginning, and I still think it was a little rustling, but the tables are turned now; Cain is in a position to crack the whip. A little free Arrowhead beef won't satisfy him; he'll want money, and Mundy will have to come through, or else."

Grumpy reared up in his chair. "That's plain as print to me! That dirty galoot is the gent to watch. We're in this case now, Buck, and we're goin' to give it plenty of attention. If we can nail Ike Cain, we can tag Mundy and stop this trouble that's comin' at Johnnie."

"You ain't advisin' me to take anybody into custody on suspicion of murder, are you?" Rainsford asked.

"That's the last thing in the world I want you to do right now," Rip told him. "We haven't got evidence enough to hold anyone. I know we haven't much time as far as Kendrick is concerned. If he'd only hold off a week or two—"

"He won't, Rip. The *Gazette* printed the rodeo program this afternoon. The race is three weeks from tomorrow. I miss my guess if he doesn't ask the judge for a hearin' in two or three days, at most. I don't know whether Dan can pull a trick out of his sleeve and get a postponement." Rainsford clapped on his hat. "I'll let you boys get to bed. You'll be seein' Dan in the mornin', of course?"

"As soon as he gets down," said Rip. "Drop around if

you can. I think we better not say anything to Johnnie about how bad things look."

"No, don't say a word," Grumpy spoke up. "He ain't lost his horse yet. You can take it for granted that Ike didn't lose any time gettin' to Mundy with a report of our bein' at Tipstone. We may have lost a trick in not layin' out and tailin' him."

"There's something in that," Rainbow acknowledged. "I wonder how he'll come down from the station to Arrowhead."

"How did you fellas come down?" Rainsford asked.

"We came through the Witch Hills."

Buck said, "Ike will travel that way, too. He knows those hills like a book. After the way you stirred things up, I imagine he'll be gittin' together with Mundy quite reg'lar to compare notes. Mundy will be leery of goin' to Tipstone, and he won't appreciate havin' Ike showin' up at the ranch. It would make talk."

"Buck, I think you've put your finger on something!" Rip snapped erect in his chair, suddenly alert. "That pair will be getting together, and Cain will make Mundy come to him." He glanced at Grumpy. "We ought to be able to spot their meeting place if we lay out in the Witch Hills for a few days. It may be hoping for too much to figure we might get close enough to get a line on what they're doing, but I haven't anything better to suggest."

"I'll go out with you," Rainsford announced. "I believe I can show you where Mundy will be goin'. Ike Cain had a cabin high in those hills before he got the station at Tipstone. I know because I had to dig him out of it the first time I arrested him. You'd have trouble findin' it by yourselves. If it's okay with you, we'll pack some grub and do a quiet sneak out of Black Forks tomorrow evenin'."

They talked it over for several minutes. Buck said goodnight, then, and started out. He came back after going down the hall a few steps.

"It just occurred to me that Stark Tremaine might know somethin' about Charlie Guthrie's missin' horse. Ellis went from the Guthries to Double Diamond and he and Tremaine were thick. You know how cowpunchers like to gas; Ellis might have said somethin' that Stark will recall. I understand the Double Diamond has begun to gather, and that he's busy. But he'd come in if you asked him. If you could git word out to him by mornin', he could be in town by early afternoon. We wouldn't have to change our plans."

"That's a good hunch," the little one declared. "Do you agree with me, Rip?"

The tall man said, "I'm all for it. But I can see that it'll put Stark in a tough spot. He may not feel that he can take sides against Resa's father. We'll put it up to him, however. Have you seen anyone in town from out that way who might be going home tonight, Buck?"

"I saw Frank Willmine earlier in the evenin'. Grumpy's half undressed. Suppose you grab your hat, Rip, and we'll see if we can catch Frank. You can write a note downstairs."

They tried the saloons and found Willmine in the Elkhorn. He was about ready to start home. He said he'd be glad to stop at Double Diamond.

Morning found the partners at Dan Messenger's office. Johnnie was just finishing his chores. As usual, he was delighted to see them.

"I stopped at the hotel on my way to work," he said. "I know Oddie Fowler, the clerk. He told me you got back last night. If you went to Bar 7, you didn't stay long."

"We went up to Tipstone, Johnnie," Rip returned, having decided on the spur of the moment that it would be best to be frank with him. The Kid's hands tightened on his broom.

"Somethin' about Steve?"

"You guessed it," Grumpy muttered confidentially. "You can keep that under yore hat. If you don't see us around for a day or two, and anybody tries to get a line on us, just tell 'em you think we've gone out to the ranch."

"I shore will," the boy promised, impressed by the fact that he was sharing a secret with them.

"Is Dan upstairs?" Rainbow asked.

Johnnie pulled out his new watch and noted the time.

"You got about four minutes to wait. Mr. Messenger always shows up by nine o'clock. Mrs. Lamb is up there. You can go in and sit down."

The partners started up the stairs, only to have the Kid stop them.

"The program was in the *Gazette* last evenin'. The entries for the stake race close on the twenty-first. The judges is the same as last year. You can read all about it in the paper."

Rainbow smiled understandingly. "We'll take care of everything in time. Don't worry about that. We'll hand them a surprise this year, Johnnie."

Rainbow and the little one had barely seated themselves when Messenger walked in.

"Come inside," he told them. "I'm anxious to hear what you've got to say."

"We saw Buck last night and talked things over with him," Grumpy volunteered. "He said he'd try to join us here."

Rip said, "Something may have come up. We won't wait for him; he's heard all this once. You had the right hunch about Kendrick. But you know we went up to Tipstone with a couple things on our mind. We came back believing they're more or less connected."

"Do I understand you to mean that the horse figured in Steve Ellis' death?" Dan was surprised and didn't attempt to dissemble it.

"Suppose you see what you make of it."

Without further ado, he and Grumpy proceeded to repeat what they had told Rainsford. When they finished, Messenger swung around in his chair and stared out of the window abstractly, mulling over what he had just heard.

"Time is what we need," Grumpy said. "Can you hold Kendrick off, Dan?"

"Yes, we can have it put off until the fall term of court by demanding a trial, but that would be playing right into his hands."

"How so?" Rip asked.

"Why, as soon as he enters a claim, Judge Carver will order the sheriff to impound the horse. Buck will have to take Champ away from Johnnie. It means he—and I might as well be honest and include the three of us—can give up any idea of putting him into the race. Our case will be pretty far down on the calendar and the race will be ancient history by the time we go to trial. That way, win or lose, Kendrick will have accomplished his purpose."

"I suppose the alternative is an informal hearing in the judge's chambers, with nobody testifying under oath." Ripley's tone was bitter. "We'd be licked before we start!"

Messenger had to admit that the outlook was not bright. "But," he added, "we'll have a chance to question Kendrick's witnesses. I agree with you, Rip, that Ellis could undoubtedly have spiked this game. But I'm not as sure as you are that he was shot to death to keep him from talking, though I admit it was a strange coincidence. I suppose I find it hard to believe because it seems incredible to me that a man like Mundy would go as far as murder on the utterly absurd theory that if he rigged up something that would make Kendrick a little surer of winning the race he'd so ingratiate himself with the old man that he'd advance his chances with Resa. . . . Oh, I know there was bad blood between Ellis and Mundy. But—"

"Dan, if you think it's absurd, turn to the criminal records; they're filled with murders that were just as stupidly motivated."

"You've got me there," Messenger acknowledged. "When Tremaine reaches town, I wish you would bring him up. I'll be in the office all afternoon. I think it was worthwhile asking him to come in. He may be able to tell us something. Of course, it'll only be hearsay; it's unlikely that he knows anything about Guthrie's colt of his own personal knowledge."

Grumpy gave him a sharp, questioning glance. "Why do you say that?"

"Stark's had a look at Champ, Grump. He was down at the corral when Kendrick showed up that afternoon and hinted he recognized the horse. I take it for granted that under those circumstances Stark would have told Johnnie about Charlie Guthrie's yearling."

Rainbow nodded. "You're right. It wouldn't have been a question of whether he saw something familiar about Champ; he'd have spoken to Johnnie or got word to you. I'm afraid he won't be much help to us."

The sheriff rapped on the door and walked in.

"I got some unpleasant news for you," he announced, slapping his hat on the desk. "The Kendricks are in town. Mundy and Ike Cain came in with them."

A momentary silence descended on the office. The little one was first to find his tongue. He pushed back his chair with an angry grating.

"By grab, the fat's in the fire now!" His voice was as rough as a file. "We ain't goin' to have time to turn around. Kendrick won't wait no longer than it takes the judge to git back."

Buck sat down heavily. "Carver's at the court house now. Got in about eight-thirty. Kendrick has seen him already. The judge has granted him a hearin'. Two o'clock this afternoon in his chambers. He's instructed me to have all interested parties present. The Kid's a minor. That means I'll have to git old Wash up to the court house, too."

"That won't be necessary," Rainbow said bluntly. "There's no point in getting Johnnie into this until we have to. It will be tough enough to speak to him when we know the decision has gone against us."

"It ain't a question of what I'd like to do," Rainsford protested. "But when the court gives me an order, I've got to carry it out. The Smileys have the horse in their possession. It's their right to him that's bein' questioned."

"Legally, that isn't true, Buck. When I bought the horse, Pete made the bill of sale out to me. I told Johnnie I would transfer it to him when I got back. We've been so busy that I haven't had it done, thank heaven." He pulled out his wallet and extracted the paper. "Here it is. Take a look at it."

"Put it away," the sheriff grumbled. "I don't have to read it; your word is good enough for me. I know the horse belongs to the Kid, but if you want to appear as the legal owner of the moment, I won't have to bother the Smileys."

"The judge will be satisfied with that explanation," Messenger told him. "If we need Johnnie this afternoon, I'll guarantee to produce him."

Grumpy wagged his head and said artlessly, "Shore!"

CHAPTER 14

THE PARTNERS ENCOUNTERED MUNDY on the street just before noon. He hesitated, as though he were going to stop, but he thought better of it and continued on his way. The light in his frosty eyes left no doubt of the enmity seething in him.

"We better not meet on a dark night and not know he's behind us," Grumpy muttered venomously. "It's gittin' late; Tremaine ought to be showin' up. He'll look for us at the hotel, first off."

They turned into the Bridger, only to be told at the desk that no one had been there. Grat Collamore sat down alongside them on the veranda.

"Can you beat this?" he asked carelessly. "I see they're all in town."

"I don't know, Grat," Rip replied. "I'm afraid we're going to need help."

Collamore fanned himself indolently and said, "You won't get it from Carver. Being such good friends with the two of you will be enough to make him lean over backwards to be fair to the other side."

The partners recognized the truth of that. It had kept them from going to the court house.

The gambler proved that he had sources of information of his own by saying, "They've been watching the Kid work out his horse. They know Black Lightning can't beat him. Kendrick's prepared to pay any claim for feed and care and breaking Champ that Dan Messenger makes. He won't squabble about the size of the bill; he wants the horse. Of course, he'll try to give the judge the idea that this action doesn't concern anything more than a cheap bronc that might be made into a fair-to-middling cow pony."

"We'll be on hand to see that he don't git away with anythin' like that," the little one observed pointedly.

Collamore subsided and had no more to say. His eyes roamed the street and his face was as impassive as stone. Noon-time came, and he got up; the dining room doors had been opened.

"Suppose you leave that end of it to me," he said woodenly. "I think I can do better than you."

The Kendricks came up the steps a few minutes later. Resa spoke to the partners. Old Pike ignored them coolly and continued on to the dining room.

"We better be goin' in, too," Grumpy advised. "It's fillin' up."

"Here comes the judge," Rip told him. "We can say hello to him, at least."

Judge Carver's manner was reserved. "I offered to disqualify myself on account of our close relations," he said. "Kendrick thought that wasn't necessary. You know I'll be impartial. It seems to be a trifling matter."

Rip thought it best to say no more. After the judge had been seated, they found a table in the dining room. Collamore sat a few feet away. On the opposite side, Resa and her father were being served. Grat's eyes strayed in their direction several times but with the same casualness with which he regarded Judge Carver and the others. He took his time over his food.

The partners were watching him. When he finished he hauled himself to his feet and sauntered over to the Kendricks and stopped.

He said, "I understand you're claiming that buckskin horse the Smiley boy's got down on flats belongs to you,

Pike." He wanted to be overheard and pitched his voice accordingly.

"I'd rather not say anything about it if it's just the same to you," Kendrick returned, his annoyance obvious. Collamore did not take the hint.

"I suppose you know he's as fast or faster than Black Lightning."

"Hunh!" Kendrick snorted scornfully. "That's ridiculous!"

"Maybe," Grat conceded lightly. "I just wanted to tell you that if you get title to him I'll be glad to take him off your hands for five hundred dollars."

The cowman's face turned purple with fury. He realized that Judge Carver and everyone in the dining room was overhearing every word of this.

"You'd be hard to find if I took you up, Collamore. You know that big bronc has been running wild and doesn't amount to anything."

"I'll make it six hundred," Grat said, with maddening equanimity. "You can have the cash or a certified check any time. What do you say?"

"You're out of your mind!" Pike sputtered. "Don't bother me with your wild talk!"

Collamore laughed. "So you know what the horse is worth. Well, you can't blame me for trying to find a bargain."

He strolled out, leaving tongues wagging.

"By grab, that stripped the sheep's clothin' off the wolf!" Grumpy declared, with a chuckle. "Look at the judge's face, Rip. Reckon he knows this matter ain't so triflin' as he allowed."

A smile of satisfaction curled Rainbow's lips. "We won't hear anything out of Kendrick this afternoon about Champ being a cheap horse."

If the partners had thought of it at all, they would have realized that Johnnie had a far too sensitive finger on the pulse of the town for Kendrick's presence, with Mundy and Ike Cain, to escape his attention for long. He was on the steps, waiting for them when they came out of the dining room. The anxiety stamped on his young face could not be concealed.

"Kendrick's here to do somethin'. I know it!"

Rainbow cast his eye over the veranda and decided there were too many listening ears. "Walk down the street with us," he said.

They went as far as Rinehart's store and stopped at the hitch rack. The Kid knew the partners well enough to find nothing reassuring in their manner.

"Johnnie, this is it, all right," Rainbow told him. "Kendrick's going to make his move this afternoon. But that's no reason for us to start falling apart. We know exactly what he's going to do and we're ready for him. I want you to go home and stay there until you hear from us."

"Shore," the boy muttered desperately. His heart was in his eyes as he looked up at them. "I can't give up Champ! I'd rather die!"

Grumpy's mouth hardened. "You ain't givin' him up, Kid. You go home as Rip says, and sit tight. You go on, now, and keep yore chin up."

After a minute or two, Johnnie trudged off in the direction of the cabin, a picture of complete dejection. The partners turned back to the Bridger, equally sober.

One-thirty passed without any sign of Tremaine.

"Reckon we can give him up," Grumpy muttered.

Rip said, "I'm afraid so. He might have been very little help to us, but anything would be better than nothing. We might as well wander up to the court house. We'll pick Dan up on the way."

Messenger found Grat Collamore's offer to buy Champ decidedly interesting. "It was a smart way of establishing the value of the horse. It won't help Kendrick any."

They found Pike and Resa in the empty court room. They had Mrs. Guthrie with them.

"We can wait out here until the judge calls us in," said Dan. "I see Buck coming."

They had been standing on the steps only a few minutes, when Joe Mundy arrived with old Ike. The latter shifted his eyes as he passed. Mundy glanced neither to right nor left. The sheriff looked into the court room and saw them take seats just back of Resa and her father.

"Almost two o'clock," he drawled. "Evidently Kendrick is goin' to go it alone. Must figger he doesn't need a lawyer."

Judge Carver's clerk opened a door at the side of the bench and beckoned for them to follow him.

"That's us," Grumpy muttered. "Let's file in."

Though the room in which the hearing was to be held bore the dignified title of the judge's chambers, it was just a box-like room, plainly furnished with a desk and chairs and the county's law library.

Judge Carver spoke to the sheriff. "Where's the boy and his father?"

Rainsford's explanation surprised him, and Pike, as well. The judge glanced at Ripley.

"I didn't realize you were a principal in this matter. I presume you are in a position to produce the horse if you are ordered to do so."

Rainbow avoided saying yes or no. "He's been held in a corral, down on the flats, for weeks, Judge. Everyone in Black Forks knows it. I'm sure Mr. Kendrick isn't in any doubt about it."

Pike started to bristle but contented himself by giving Rip a stormy glance. Under the judge's questioning the owner of Arrowhead quickly established his purchase of the Guthrie ranch, with all rights and title to anything pertaining thereto.

What he had to say regarding the disappearance of a buckskin yearling from the Guthrie place was only what the partners and Messenger expected.

"Mrs. Guthrie will confirm what I've said," he finished.

The old woman's statement was equally unsurprising.

"You recall losing the horse to which Mr. Kendrick refers?" Carver asked.

"It's jest as Pike tells it," she said. "Charlie was sick abed and couldn't go after the colt. He allus figgered it was out on the desert, runnin' with the wild ones."

"How long ago was this, Mrs. Guthrie?"

"Three years ago," she answered, without a moment's hesitation.

Dan leaped to his feet. "I'd like to question Mrs. Guthrie on that point, Judge."

Carver nodded, and Messenger turned to the old woman.

"Mrs. Guthrie, you've changed your story in the last twenty-four hours. Has anyone coached you regarding the statements you are making here?"

"The idear! I know my own mind, Mr. Messenger!"

"I presume you knew it yesterday," Dan returned pointedly. "Mr. Ripley and Mr. Gibbs were at your place about noon. You told them Steve Ellis was working for you when the horse disappeared; and you placed the time as the spring before your husband died. Your husband has been dead three years, and Ellis worked for Double Diamond for twelve to fourteen months after leaving you. That adds up to four years. If the horse was a yearling when he broke away, he'd be five years old now. Both of your stories can't be true—or do you deny having made these statements yesterday?"

Mrs. Guthrie had begun to fidget in her chair. She sent an appealing glance in Kendrick's direction. "I don't know what I told those men yesterday," she declared nervously. "I was confused when they was there—I was packing up. Without thinkin', I may have said it was the spring before Charlie passed away. If I did, I was wrong; it was the spring he was so sick, jest afore he died. Steve had left us and we was there alone."

Dan knew she was lying, but he couldn't shake her revised story. He said, "I wish I had you under oath, Mrs. Guthrie. I believe I could make you tell a different story." He checked himself as he was about to sit down. "When you sold out to Mr. Kendrick, did you have an idea of the value of the missing horse?"

"Why, I knew he was an awful good colt. I—"

"It might interest you to know that Mr. Kendrick was offered six hundred dollars for the horse he claims to be your buckskin."

The old woman's eyes snapped vindictively at old Pike. She had received from him only a few hundred dollars more for everything she had sold.

"It wasn't a legitimate offer," Kendrick hastened to tell her, afraid lest she blurt out the truth. Judge Carver's eyes bored into him sternly.

"It sounded legitimate to me," he remarked. "No one has ever accused Collamore of throwing his money away." With the pertinence Rip and Grumpy had come to expect from him, he added, "I don't suppose you would part with Black Lightning for six hundred dollars."

Pike squirmed and assured Mrs. Guthrie that if his claim were allowed he would make an adjustment with her.

"That's just the same as bribin' the witness, ain't it, Judge?" Grumpy spoke up. "I never heard of Pike Kendrick tossin' his money away, either."

Carver frowned. "I'm not interested in the degree of Mr. Kendrick's generosity." His glance went to Dan. "Since you are representing Rainbow, I'll address myself to you. You've heard Mrs. Guthrie state that a buckskin yearling disappeared from their ranch. Have you anything to offer that would disprove that statement?"

"No, Judge. We're quite willing to concede that such an animal broke away from the Guthrie place. We deny only the inference that the horse Rainbow bought from Pete Smith is that animal, and the correctness of the date Mrs. Guthrie gives. It is a very important point. We contend that the story she told yesterday was the true one, making the missing colt five years old. The horse known as Champ is only four. Mr. Kendrick has been careful to learn as much. It warrants the suspicion that pressure has been brought to bear on the witness to make her change her story to conform with that fact."

"Have you any evidence to that effect?"

Dan had to say no.

"Have you any witnesses, or evidence, to support your argument that it was four years ago the horse broke away?"

"We expected to be able to offer a witness. We sent

word to him last night, Judge. It evidently failed to reach him."

Judge Carver straightened up at his desk and weighed what he was about to say. "In the absence of any evidence to the contrary, I am compelled to accept Mrs. Guthrie's story," he began. "I know of my own knowledge that horses that go wild invariably find their way out to the Red Desert and run with the bands of so-called broomtails. I take it there is no question that the horse Pete Smith sold to Rainbow was trapped on the desert."

"We don't dispute that," said Dan. "I—" The door behind him had opened, and Tremaine stood there. "Here is our missing witness, now, Judge. . . . Come in, Stark!"

CHAPTER 15

IKE CAIN WAS THE ONLY ONE to evince no interest as Tremaine walked into the room. Mundy left his seat and went over to Kendrick immediately and whispered something in his ear. Resa lost her air of boredom at once. As for the judge, he settled back with what appeared to be conscious relief.

"I was up beyond Haystack Peak when your message got to me, Rip," Stark explained. "I got here as quickly as I could. . . . What's this all about?"

"I think Judge Carver is the one to tell you," Messenger suggested.

"Just a minute!" Kendrick burst out excitedly. He fastened his irate eye on Tremaine. "I don't know what you're here to say, but I'm telling you plainly, Tremaine, that if you side against me, you'll never put foot on Arrowhead again!"

"Father!" Resa cried, aghast. "You and Joe led me to believe it was the truth you were after! If Stark can shed any light on this matter, he should speak, by all means!"

"I'll thank you to keep out of this!" old Pike snapped.

"I'd welcome unprejudiced evidence, but Tremaine is hand in glove with the bunch that's been making all this to-do over the Kid. He can decide now which side of the bread his butter is on!"

"I refuse to be silenced," Resa said tensely, the blood draining away from her cheeks. "If Johnnie's horse doesn't belong to you, surely you don't want him, Father." She turned to Tremaine. "If you have anything to say, Stark, I insist that you speak."

"I'm still in the dark," he told her. "If the Judge will give me an idea of what's wanted of me, I'll be glad to oblige."

"Be seated," Carver told him, "and I'll explain what we are trying to decide." It required only a few moments, and he then turned to Messenger. "You may proceed."

Dan began by asking Stark if he recalled the spring when Steve Ellis joined the Double Diamond crew.

"Certainly," was the ready response. "It was four years ago."

"In your conversations with Ellis, did he ever have anything to say about a buckskin yearling that broke away from the Guthrie ranch? Take your time about answering and tell us exactly what he said."

Tremaine sat there in a deepening silence, with everyone in the room hanging on his answer. They saw him shake his head.

"I'm sorry," he said, "but to the best of my knowledge Steve never said anything."

It was a blow to the hopes of the partners and Messenger. Across the room, Buck Rainsford's face was dark with disappointment. They knew Tremaine had not been cowed by anything Kendrick had said.

"Are you positive, Stark?" Dan demanded peremptorily.

"I've got to say yes. Steve often spoke of Charlie Guthrie, but he never mentioned anything about a horse that had gone wild."

Mundy and Ike relaxed, and Kendrick was openly jubilant.

"Of course he couldn't have said anything," he exclaimed. "The colt didn't get away till after Ellis went to work for your outfit." He swung around to Cain. "Ike, you tell the Judge what you know about the horse and how you identified him."

"Wal—"

"Wait, Ike," Judge Carver interjected admonishingly. "I want to warn you that your veracity doesn't rate very high with me. I don't want any long-winded dissertation from you. Stick to facts, and be sure you state them correctly."

"Wal, Jedge, they ain't no reason for me to lie about this. It ain't my hoss they're wranglin' over. I knew all about the y'arlin' bustin' away. I was up thar to the ranch onct er twicest when it was jest a young colt." Ike crossed his spindly legs and glanced over the room nonchalantly.

"Was Steve Ellis working there at the time?" Carver inquired.

"No, Jedge, Charlie was alone and bed-ridden most o' the time." He caught Grumpy glaring at him and pulled his eyes away quickly.

"Continue, Ike!" Carver prompted.

"Wal, Jedge, the colt had an accident; cut his right ear on some barbed wire. It healed up all right but it musta hurt the cord. When he'd raise his ears after that, the tip o' the right one would fall over. What you call a lop ear. Charlie felt bad about it. It was the only blemish on the hoss."

"And you've found the same mark on Champ?"

"Absolutely, Jedge! No question about it! Pike asked me to come in and have a look at the hoss. I spotted that ear right off."

"The lyin' old buzzard!" Grumpy muttered under his breath to Rainbow. "Champ's right ear does lop over a bit, Rip. We'll never beat this frame-up. You keep the talk going; give me thirty minutes."

The tall man's face remained inscrutable as the little one tip-toed to the door and stepped out.

"What's your answer to the allegation, Mr. Messenger?" Carver inquired soberly.

"I'd like to confer with Rainbow a moment, Judge." The permission was given. Dan walked to the rear of the room with Rip.

"It looks as though this thing is going against us," he said grimly. "There is something wrong with Champ's right ear. Cain has simply rigged his story to fit the circumstances. I believe the Judge knows the man is lying. But that isn't going to help us any; if we can't prove Ike is lying, Carver will have to accept his story."

Through the window Rainbow saw Grumpy hail a passing rig and climb in hurriedly. The driver turned his team and drove off in the direction of the flats.

"If we keep Cain talking long enough, he may trip himself," the tall man suggested. "It seems to be our only chance. If I lose, I've still got a claim against Kendrick for feed and care. Run it up as high as you can. It'll be something for Johnnie."

The hearing ground on. Rip had conceded defeat and his thoughts were riding with Grumpy.

Johnnie had been at the cabin door for an hour, and he saw the little man running up the path, the look on his face leaving no doubt as to the nature of his news.

A cry of anguish was wrung from the boy that brought his father to the door. Mr. Smiley had been unable to contain himself from the moment Johnnie had told him what was taking place at the court house. He tore off his dark glasses. Straining his eyes, he saw that it was the little one who was dashing up to the cabin.

"Great day in the morning!" he screeched. "Don't tell me that hoss-thief Kendrick is takin' Champ away from my boy!"

"Wash, shut yore mouth!" Grumpy snapped. "I want to talk to Johnnie, and I got to be quick about it!" He glared fiercely at the Kid. "Now you listen to me and you git every word of what I say, and git it straight! This thing at the court house is goin' ag'in us, but you ain't lost Champ yet, and you won't if you do exactly what I tell you. You toss yore saddle on him in a hurry. Yore pa and me will git some grub together for you. I want you to light out of here for the north. Go right out east on the flats till yo're four, five miles beyond town. You head for the Witch Hills, then. You understand?"

The Kid nodded, trying to get a grip on himself.

"When you hit the hills, hole up somewhere for a day," Grumpy continued inflexibly, "then move on and hole up again for another day. Do the same thing the third day. You'll be leavin' some sign behind you, horse droppin's and the like for a good trailer like Buck to pick up. He'll be out lookin' for you, Kid, and so will Mundy. Make yore camps so they'll git the idea yo're workin' out to the desert. On the fourth day, you line out straight for the Bar 7 round-up. Tell Trilling Rip and me sent you. Turn yore horse into the round-up remuda. It'll be the last place anyone will be lookin' for you. You can keep yore eyes open. If you see anyone showin' up, make yoreself scarce. And remember this, no one but Rainsford can take Champ away from you, should anybody catch up with you."

"What about Pappy?" Johnnie jerked out, a catch in his throat. "He can't take care of himself."

"I'll git somebody down here to look after him. You got nothin' to worry about on that score. You stick with the wagon till we show up. Time's all we need to bust this rotten business wide open. You start steppin', Johnnie! I want you away from here in five minutes!"

It took a minute or two longer than that, but the Kid had been gone a quarter of an hour when the little man heard voices outside.

"They're comin'," he warned Mr. Smiley. "You keep yore lip buttoned, Wash. You ain't got the least idea where the boy's lit out for."

He saw Kendrick and Mundy, accompanied by the sheriff and Rainbow moving along the path.

Rainsford had a premonition of what they were to find, and his glance went to the empty corral. The expression on his poker face did not change. Kendrick barged past him into the cabin.

"So, this is where you dodged to!" Pike ripped out

suspiciously on catching sight of Grumpy. "I might have known it! Where's the Kid and the horse?"

"Gone for a little ride, I reckon," was the unperturbed answer. "How did the judge decide, Pike?"

"In my favor! Rainsford's got his orders."

"That's too bad," Grumpy purred. He looked up at the sheriff. "Looks like you might have some waitin' to do, Buck. It may be some time before the Kid gets back."

Mundy decided that it was time for him to take a hand. "If you think you can conceal the horse, you won't get away with it, Gibbs!" he rapped out threateningly. "A court order has been issued, and you'll obey or you and the Kid will both be in trouble!"

"Wal, that comes a little late," Grumpy murmured innocently. "There wa'n't any court order in existence when the boy left, or I would have advised him differently. Fact is, I didn't think there was any chance that you highbinders could pull the wool over the judge's eyes."

Kendrick had turned his attention to Mr. Smiley.

"What have you got to say?" he demanded wrathfully. "You know where the Kid is!"

"Wal, the fact is, I don't, Pike," the old man cackled, with surprising impudence. "He was travelin' awful fast when he left here."

"This has gone far enough," Buck said with authority. "It means I'll have to go after him. And I won't need any assistance," he added, giving Mundy a meaningful glance.

Kendrick's usually ruddy face had taken on an apoplectic hue.

"I won't stand for no trickery, Rainsford!" he bellowed. "I know where your sympathies lie! That horse belongs to me, and I mean to have him!" He swung around on Rainbow, his eyes blazing. "You were a party to this conniving. Carver's order calls on you to deliver the animal to me. You'll do it or suffer the consequences!"

"Mr. Kendrick, if it's my money you want," Rip answered with infuriating calmness, "I'm ready to settle with you now."

"No you don't!" Pike flared back. "I don't want your money! I want the horse!"

Rainbow nodded. "Don't go too far in your anxiety to get your hands on him," he advised. "You might tell your foreman to be equally careful."

Mundy was forced to take it up.

"You may drag a lot of weight around here, Ripley, but don't expect me to run when you bark. Your loose talk up at Tipstone yesterday got back to me. I wish I'd been there."

"So do I," the tall man said quietly, drilling him with his gray eyes. "I don't know where the Kid is. But I don't want to hear that he's been messed up again by you. If I do, you'll find I'm a little quicker on the draw than Ellis."

Kendrick stopped the argument before it got out of hand, and after another blistering demand for action by the sheriff, he and Mundy left. Rainsford stood there, rolling his shoulders.

"This is a fine spot you boys put me in. I don't mind Kendrick's rantin' but I'd almost as soon turn in my badge as to go out and drag that boy in with his horse and see it turned over to that yappin' hyena!"

"Wal, you can let yore conscience be yore guide, Buck," Grumpy piped up. "You don't have to look around every corner you pass."

CHAPTER 16

RAINSFORD RODE HIMSELF WEARY in the next few days. He knew Johnnie and Champ had to have water; and the boy would have to have food carried out to him or be in a position to come in for it.

The one place not to look, Buck felt, was the partners' range beyond Bar 7. Seeing that Grumpy had arranged the escape from town, it seemed altogether unlikely that he wouldn't have thought of something better than that. In lesser degree, and for the same reason, the sheriff regarded Bar 7 itself as unlikely hunting-ground. There was Double Diamond, with the Kid's friend Tremaine in virtual charge of its sprawling range. It was enough to take Buck there first. He questioned Harley Purcell, the owner of the brand, Stark and half a dozen punchers. They convinced him that they had seen nothing of Johnnie. He rode on, and in the Witch Hills he found the Kid's first camp. It was deep in a willow brake. He could see that the boy had stretched a rope and made a temporary corral.

Rainsford slept there and took up the trail in the morning. He found the second camp, and then the third, but Johnnie was never less than a day ahead of him. That night the sheriff rode into Arrowhead for supper and a bed.

Mundy and Pike were together on the gallery when Buck stepped down from his jaded horse. They were full of questions.

"He's either through or still in the Witch Hills," he told them. "These phantom corrals I'm chasin' don't git me very far."

"He's making for the desert," Mundy asserted. "I figured he would."

"It looks that way," Buck agreed, though he thought otherwise. He couldn't believe that Grumpy wouldn't have warned Johnnie against making that mistake. "He may be right here on Arrowhead," he continued, to their surprise. "He had some good friends in your crew, Pike."

Kendrick's glance went to his foreman. "What've you got to say to that, Joe?" His tone had a sharp edge of criticism. "I know you and some of the old hands don't hit it off too well, but I'm damned if I thought there was any chance of a double-cross."

"There's nothing to it," Mundy returned flatly. "I can pick out the men Rainsford is referring to. If you say so, I'll bring them in in the morning and we can question them."

"No," Buck objected, "we wouldn't git anythin' out of 'em that way. Where you workin'?"

"The south range."

"I'll ride down there in the mornin' and do my own questionin'."

Arrowhead was a pleasant place. A creek flowed across the ranch yards, keeping the grass green and giving the poplars and cottonwoods a luxuriant growth. The bunk houses, crew's kitchen and the corrals were located at the end of the yard, and the house was so situated that the home life of the ranch could be observed from the gallery.

Resa came out, after Mundy had left. She asked about Johnnie. Her father invited her to sit down with them. She said no, and in a minute or two, excused herself and turned back into the house. Pike let his pipe go out and sat there in moody silence.

"I went too far with her the other day in town," he confessed. "I shouldn't have jumped Tremaine the way I did." He shook his head. "It's a strange thing, Rainsford; that Smiley boy worked here for a spell and now the whole life of this ranch seems to be revolving around him. I wish I'd never laid eyes on the Kid!"

"I don't know, Pike," the sheriff muttered dubiously. "You're tryin' awful hard to play Simon Legree, but right down inside of you, I don't believe you mean it."

"I mean to win the stake race," was the flinty response.

"There could be more important things," said Rainsford. "But it appears that you've got the Kid euchred out of it. If he shows his face, you grab his horse, and if he keeps on the dodge, he can't enter him in any race."

Pike scowled. "You find him. I'm not taking any chances with Ripley and Gibbs pulling a trick on me at the last minute."

Buck questioned Reb Justin and Happy Sherdell, Johnnie's particular cronies, the next morning. They seemed to be as well informed as to what had taken place in town as though they had read a detailed account of it in some newspaper. They insisted, however, that they neither knew nor had seen anything of the Kid.

"Mundy's been lookin' for him," Happy volunteered. "He's got Pasco and Lesant out around Sioux Rocks, combin' that country."

"Yeh, and he's been doin' some lookin' on his own account," Reb chimed in. "He's been leavin' the work most every afternoon. Mebbe he just comes into the house, but that ain't what we think. He's got somethin' on his mind."

Rainsford found this information more interesting than he let on. A man who knew his way could leave Arrowhead's south range in the late afternoon and be at Ike Cain's old cabin in the Witch Hills by dark. With the thought resting heavily on him, Buck returned to the hills and took up the Kid's trail where he had dropped it the previous evening. He followed it until noon, when it faded completely. Johnnie and Champ seemed to have picked up their heels and taken off through the air.

There wasn't any doubt in Buck's mind but what the Kid had traveled along the rocks on the crest of the ridge. He couldn't find where the boy had left them, however. He was singularly undisturbed over it. With the afternoon before him, he came off the ridge and doubled back on his own trail for several miles. After pausing to orient himself, he turned off sharply to his left and began picking his way through rough, broken country that made the going slow.

Years had passed since he had had any occasion to find Ike Cain's old cabin, but he continued to find out-croppings and down timber that looked familiar. When the hills began to pinch up higher abruptly, he knew he wasn't mistaken. He picked up a faint trail a few minutes later and decided it had been used recently. He followed it, moving cautiously, and it led him to the tumbledown cabin. After watching it from a distance until he was sure there was no one there, he came up, then, and found plentiful evidence that it had been visited within the last few days.

His first thought was to conceal himself and his horse and sit tight, but knowing he might have to wait a day or two, or even three, for developments, and being without food, convinced him it would be foolish. Instead, he decided to head for the Bar 7 house, spend the night there and outfit himself with grub enough to last him a week, after which he would swing across the partners' range and down through Bar 7, looking for the Kid, and back to the Witch Hills.

It was a long ride to Bar 7, and the shadows were falling when he rode in. He was surprised to have Grumpy hail him before he could get down.

"Thought you was in town," Buck called back, not without suspicion.

"Rip and I just came up to git some horses and our own ridin' gear. You havin' any luck?"

"Not with the hand you dealt me," Buck declared dryly. "The Kid seems to have taken wings. You and Rip here alone?"

"Yeh, haven't even got a cook. Rip's out in the kitchen, seein' what he can rustle up. Come on in!"

When Rainsford told the partners what he had discovered in the Witch Hills, it definitely relegated any talk about Johnnie and Champ to second place. There was no question in their minds as to who had been at the cabin recently.

"I'm ready to forget about the Kid for a few days and go back there with you and hang on till somethin' cracks," said Buck. "We can leave here in the mornin' and work our way in without much chance of bein' spotted. It'll take us longer to find a safe place to hide out our broncs than anythin' else."

They packed the food they were likely to need in gunnysacks and got a small bag of oats for the horses before going to bed. It enabled them to get an early start. Though by midmorning Rainsford was able to state that they were within three miles of the cabin, noon had come and gone before they caught their first glimpse of it.

"Any water in here?" Rainbow asked, after studying the terrain carefully with a pair of glasses.

"Springs," Buck replied. "We ought to find one without any trouble. We're certainly goin' to need water."

"The grass is still green on that slope beyond the cabin." Rip handed the glasses to Rainsford. "Take a look. I don't know what's on the other side of that hogback, but I suggest we circle over that way; we may find water and a good place to leave the horses. If we do, we'll be in position to work down through the backbrush almost to the door."

They made the detour and were rewarded by finding a flowing spring and a sheltered spot. Grumpy climbed the intervening ridge and found himself looking down on the shack.

"Ain't a bad climb at all," he announced, on getting back. "During the middle of the day it ought to be safe to light a fire down in here and boil some coffee." He glanced at the sun. "It's time to eat right now."

They crossed the saddle and crawled down through the brush in the late afternoon.

"This ought to be close enough," the little one observed. "We don't have to look down their throats to catch what they're sayin'."

"That's right," Buck agreed. "If they come, it'll be in the early evenin'. We can close in then if we find it necessary."

It was the beginning of a long and apparently fruitless vigil. After two days and nights of it even Rainbow's patience began to wear thin.

"I say let's stick it out another twenty-four hours," he argued. "We know they've been here once or twice; there's reason to believe they'll come again."

"We'll sit it out another night, but that's all," Rainsford told him. "I'm goin' down and see about some breakfast. You boys come along when you're ready."

"We'll go along with you now," the little one spoke up. "It's goin' to be hot ag'in in this brush around noon. No point in bakin' our brains out like we did the last two days."

"I don't object to taking it easy," said Rip. "If we're back here by five it'll be early enough."

They got through another long, tedious day, and in the afternoon took up their position in the brush. The sun dropped behind the hills and the purple haze of evening had begun to deepen, when Grumpy reached out and put a warning hand on Rainbow's leg. A shabby figure on horseback was moving toward the cabin from the east. Buck nodded in answer to the tall man's nudge.

"It's Ike," he muttered.

Cain rode up to the door and dropped the reins over his bronc's head. He glanced inside but found no reason to enter the old shack. His confident manner suggested that it had not occurred to him that he might not be alone in these hills. He had a gun on his hip. He broke it open, made sure it was loaded and in working condition, as a man might who expected to have some need of a gun, before he returned it to the holster and sat down on a log.

Cain seemed to reach the end of his patience after he had smoked several cigarettes. He got to his feet three or four times and peered off to the west. Finally, he was rewarded. A horseman was coming up the trail Rainsford had used when he found the cabin. It was Joe Mundy. He rode up to Cain. "I couldn't get it, Ike," he said from the saddle. "The old man wouldn't let me have it."

It took no more to throw Cain into a violent rage.

"I ain't lookin' to Kendrick fer my money!" he ripped out. "Yo're the gent I did my dickerin' with; an' I told yuh the last time I wa'n't standin' fer no more stallin'!"

Mundy got down, his rocky face hard but otherwise outwardly undisturbed by Ike's outburst.

"You'll have to take it easy," he said flatly. "You've had fifty bucks already. No reason for you to be squawking; we haven't got the horse yet."

Cain brushed this aside wrathfully.

"It wa'n't my fault the hoss was run out on yuh! Don't try to come that on me, Mundy! I lied myself blue in the face fer yuh!"

"And you damn near bungled everything at the last minute!" Mundy's voice began to rumble sullenly. "What do you think would have happened to your story if Tremaine had been able to say anything?"

"Huh!" Ike snorted. "How could Steve have told him

anythin' about a buckskin y'arlin' when there wa'n't no
sech animal? It was a sorrel mare Guthrie lost; I had to
talk myself hoarse convincin' Hattie it was a buckskin. I
ain't tellin' yuh nothin' yuh didn't know! Steve Ellis was
the only one who coulda done any talkin'. That's why you
cut him down."

Mundy's neck muscles corded and the icy glitter that
touched his eyes was ominous.

"I'm getting sick of having you reminding me of cer-
tain things every time we meet! You want to stop cracking
the whip, Ike!"

In the afterglow, they stood out in sharp silhouette to
the partners and Rainsford. Ike kept his hands hanging
loosely at his sides. The care with which he had made sure
of his gun suggested that he was not going to be caught
unawares.

"We better not wait any longer," Rainbow said quietly.
"We've got enough to send Mundy away for keeps."

Buck nodded and raised his rifle. He said, "When I call
out for 'em to freeze, you and Grump git their guns."

"Yuh don't have to tell me I may know too much for
my own health," Ike was growling. "That occurred to me
some time back. It'll make me right kereful. The bank's
tryin' to toss me out of Tipstone. I gotta do sunthin' for
'em, and I'm lookin' to yuh fer it. I got till the fifteenth.
. . . Yuh don't want to disappoint me, Mundy!"

The threat had no sooner been uttered than the Arrowhead foreman went for his gun. Cain was barely a second
behind him. But they were too late.

"Start reachin'!" Rainsford cried. "I got my rifle centered on you!"

Grumpy darted out of the brush, his gun in his fist, and
disarmed the two bewildered men. Only when the sheriff
snapped on the handcuffs did Mundy shake himself out of
his trance.

"I'm arrestin' you for the murder of Steve Ellis," Buck
drawled. "I'm taking you in, too, Ike. Maybe you can turn
State's evidence and save your rotten hide."

Mundy seized the moment to fling himself at his horse in

a desperate attempt to escape. Rip stuck out a foot and tripped him, and he pitched headlong into a clump of sagebrush.

Buck hauled him to his feet.

"I'll tap you on the head if you've got anythin' else like that on your mind!" he growled.

Grumpy had not taken his eyes off Ike Cain.

"Yuh don't have to wave that gun in my face!" Ike whined. "I'll do plenty talkin' when the time comes."

"Lop ear, eh?" the little man rapped. "I'll give you a pair of 'em if you so much as bat an eye-winker!"

"I want to git out of here before black night," Buck said to the partners. "I don't need you boys to help me git this pair into town. If you just happen to know where the Kid can be found, you better git to him; Kendrick can't touch Champ now."

CHAPTER 17

RAINBOW AND GRUMPY HAD HIRED Andy McBain, an old-time puncher, to look after the Kid's father. Andy had long since been reduced to swamping out bunkhouses and helping out in ranch kitchens, and he was glad to get the work. He and Mr. Smiley had been cronies for years, and the arrangement had worked out so well that the latter objected strenuously when the partners suggested that Andy's services were no longer required.

"It ain't human, figgerin' to leave me alone down here jest when everybody in this town is enjoyin' 'emselves!" he stormed. "Andy and me was gittin' along like two bugs in a rug!"

"What do you mean, alone?" Grumpy demanded. "You got Johnnie back."

"Yeh, but he'll be takin' Champ out to the rodeo grounds next week and roostin' there with him. Won't be a soul botherin' about me."

"All right," Rip told him, "Andy can stay till the race is over. You don't mind, Grump?"

"No, I don't suppose I do. But yo're a hard man to argue with, Wash! First, you pin us down to agreein' to let you take in the races and what not, and then you pull this on us. You know you shouldn't go out in the sunlight. You won't see nothin' of the races or the buckin'."

"No, by jinks, I won't see much, but I can sit in the grandstand and fill up on peanuts and hear the crowd yellin'. That'll be somethin'." He smacked his lips contemplatively. "Them rodeo fellers allus has them big, double-jointed Californy peanuts."

The partners had posted the entrance money for Johnnie. Grat Collamore had responded by making Champ a slight favorite in the betting odds. The Kid was literally walking on air. He gave the sheriff credit for being partially responsible for bringing Mundy to justice for killing Steve Ellis, and in lesser degree for establishing his right to Champ. But he really was only being generous to Buck, for deep inside of him he was convinced that Rainbow and Grumpy had done it all. They had justified his faith in them a hundred-fold.

The Kid was working Champ every morning now. The partners timed him repeatedly. The big horse continued to run the three furlongs under forty seconds. One crisp morning, with the boy pressing him, he came in a fraction of a second under thirty-nine.

"Don't crowd him after this," Rip advised. "He's ready. We don't want him to go stale."

"I'll see he don't," the boy promised. "I ain't goin' to have him leave his race down here on the flats. Have you spoken for a stable at the track?"

"Yeh, got number seven," Grumpy answered. "That's a lucky number, Kid. Bar 7 will be in town tomorrow with the beef cut. As soon as the boys git through loadin', we'll git Howie Hallett and Willis lined up to go out and stay with you."

They helped Johnnie to put a blanket on Champ. It was a new one, the gift of Grat Collamore. The boy had been reluctant to admit he was mistaken about Grat. Rip had made his realize how much they owed their success to the man.

Black Forks had begun to take on a holiday air for the rodeo and races. The big outfits had been driving in for the past week. The shipping pens gave up clouds of dust as the cattle were put aboard the cars for Omaha and Chicago. The men worked with a will, spurred on by the promise of a big time in town. Double Diamond's wagon had been first to pull into the campgrounds along the creek. There were upwards of a dozen wagons there now. The road into town lay between them and the Smiley cabin, but their cook fires cast a red glow over the flats in the evening that could be seen from the door.

The arrest of Mundy and Ike Cain had caused a sensation. But it had run its course; the two men were lodged in jail and could be forgotten temporarily. Cain had made a full confession to Perry Ashforth, the district attorney, but he was being held as a material witness.

"Reckon the judge has cooled off sufficient to make it safe for us to have it out with him," Grumpy suggested, as he and Rip returned to town from the flats.

The tall man put on a straight face and said, "You're the one who's in hot water. But I'll go along with you."

They found Judge Carver in his chambers. Ashforth was with him. He frowned forbiddingly at sight of the partners. He knew how to "throw the book at a man," and he proceeded to give them a dressing down.

"But I didn't conceal the horse, Judge," the little one protested. "He was there for anybody to see who came along."

"You showed little respect for this court," Carver insisted. "It's fortunate for you that the matter turned out the way it did."

Ashforth left, and when the door had closed on him, the judge's manner changed abruptly. "That was for his benefit," he explained. "But it was a dangerous trick to play on me, Grumpy. I suppose I'll survive it. . . . What about this horse Champ? Is it safe to place a little bet on him?"

Rainbow grinned. "A horse race is a horse race, Judge. I never bet on them, myself, but Champ just did the three-eighths in thirty-eight and a half. I don't believe any time like that was ever made in Wyoming."

"I'll risk fifty dollars," Carver declared. "I was just talking with Ashforth about the Mundy trial. I've decided not to sit on it. You'll be important witnesses, and there are other reasons why I'm going to step aside. Kendrick has been in to see me. It's been a blow to him. He insists he believed Cain's story about the Guthrie colt was true. Mundy came to him with it and he didn't question it."

"I believe that's correct," said Rip. "Of course, old Pike saw it was a way out for him and he was ready to close his eyes. Has Buck been able to pick up Pasco and Lesant?"

"No, he believes they've left the country. But Ashforth's got an airtight case without them. Zach will reach town sometime tomorrow with the drive. He tells me your stuff grades up fine."

"It should, Judge—and thanks to you. It was Bar 7 stock originally. With your permission, we'll ask Howie and Snuffy to go out to the grounds and stay with Johnnie."

The judge nodded. "They'll like it and it'll keep them out of mischief."

The professional trick ropers, riders and other performers, who followed the rodeo circuit for a living were not due to arrive in Black Forks until the end of the week, but the local talent, bronc busters and bulldoggers, had begun to register at the temporary office the Rodeo Association had opened in the Bridger House. Flags and banners had been strung across the main street, and the Black Forks Cornet Band was practicing every evening at the opera house. The sour notes floating out through the windows made it abundantly clear that practice was what the band needed.

Trilling and the Bar 7 crew had to hold their steers on the flats for over two hours the next day before they could get into the shipping pens. The partners and the judge started for the railroad as soon as word came up that the way was clear. They found Frank Dunn, the stock buyer, at the depot. He bought cattle for the feed lots in eastern Nebraska, where they were fattened for slaughter. Carver had been selling his cut to him for several years, Dunn's responsibility beginning as soon as the steers were loaded.

"Arrowhead held us up a little, Judge," he said. "Pike did his best, but he misses Mundy at a time like this. He doesn't seem to have found anyone to take his place."

"Have you seen our stuff, Frank?" Rainbow inquired.

"Yes, I went out on the flats half an hour ago and looked it over. Nice clean stock, every head of it. It'll bring top price."

In a few minutes, the cattle were pouring into the pens. The partners and the judge braved the dust with Dunn and went out on the catwalk. The long drive had taken most of the spookiness out of the steers, but their bellowing made the air tremble. Judge Carver got Trilling's attention.

"It's getting late," he shouted, cupping his hands to his mouth to make himself heard above the din. "Are you going to be able to wind it up by dark?"

"Yes, if Frank will see that his men keep spotting us to the cars!"

"I won't hold you up!" Dunn told him. "I want this stuff to roll east tonight!"

The long, hard job began. After watching the work for a few minutes Carver said he'd had enough.

"I guess we have, too," said Rip. "I'll tell Howie we want to see Snuffy and him tonight, then we'll go back to town with you."

The partners were seated on the hotel steps that evening, unable to find a vacant chair on the veranda, when Howie came looking for them.

"Snuff's in the barbershop gettin' his hair cut," he explained. "He'll be along in a couple minutes."

Rainbow told him what they wanted. The Bar 7 rider agreed readily.

"When's the Kid takin' Champ out to the grounds?" he asked.

"We want you to take him out in the middle of the mornin'," Grumpy answered. "Show up with an extry bronc for the Kid, so he can ride out with you. Black Lightnin' and most of the other horses are there already. You keep yore eye on Champ, Howie. I ain't got no reason to think anythin's goin' to go wrong, but things happen."

They were still talking, when Willis joined them. After listening to what the partners had to say, he mentioned what they were going to need.

"We'll take care of that end of it," the little one assured him. "We'll have Rinehart's send out hay and buckets and the like. You'll have to rustle yore own meals. Some canned stuff will take care of that. We'll be out reg'lar to see how yo're makin' out. And by the way, boys, if you've got any idea of gittin' oiled a little, tend to it tonight."

When Johnnie finished his chores for Messenger the next morning it was for the last time until after the race had been run. He had arranged with Andy McBain to do his work while he was away.

"He's a little slow, Mr. Messenger, but he cleans up real neat. I hope you'll be able to git along without me."

"We'll do our best," Dan said smilingly. "It will be for only a few days." The boy's face was tense with an excitement he could not conceal. "Have you found out who is going to ride Black Lightning for Kendricks?"

"Ray Eagen, from Green River. I rode against him last year."

"I remember," Dan recalled. "He knows all the tricks, Johnnie. You want to look out for him."

"I got my race planned, Mr. Messenger," the Kid declared seriously. "I'm going to take Champ out in front as quick as I can and keep him there. At that distance, he's strong enough to hold any pace he sets; I don't have to worry about a stretch drive."

He was on his way out to the rodeo ground an hour later. It was a proud moment for him when he rode down the main street of Black Forks, with Howie and Snuffy lead-ing Champ, dressed up in his new blanket.

Their arrival at the stables caused a stir among the handlers and owners of the other horses. All this attention was wine to the Kid and he more than held his own in the badinage that was leveled at him. In his imagination, he had lived every moment of this pre-race atmosphere.

The partners found Champ comfortably settled in his stable by the time they got out.

"Looks like you've made yoreselves right at home," Grumpy observed. "Have you got everything you need?"

"Everythin' but a coffee pot," Snuffy Willis told him. "How did you overlook that?"

"We figgered you could find a tin can," the little one replied, with a chuckle. "We'll git you a coffee pot."

His and Rip's particular concern at the moment was how Champ was behaving. The big horse was undeniably nervous. The boy read their thought.

"He's scared a little, but he ain't actin' up," he said. "I knew he wouldn't. I'm goin' to jog him around the track a couple times. He'll git the feel o' things purty quick."

The partners watched him circle the track.

"I dunno," Grumpy muttered dubiously.

"You don't know what?" Rainbow's tone was uncon-sciously sharp.

"How he's goin' to act when he faces a crowd and that dang band! He'll lose if he's left at the post; the distance is too short for him to come on and win after a bad start."

"That's a pleasant thought," Rip observed sarcastically. "If you want to carry anything like that around with you, go to it. I'm not going to do it; I believe Champ will come through."

That ended it for the time being, but it popped up in their conversations with Rainsford and Messenger re-peatedly.

"I think you're worryin' yourself needlessly, Grump," Buck said, the evening before the race. He had been going out to the track every day. "From what I saw this after-

noon, it looked to me as though Black Lightnin' and that
new horse of Ira Bushfield's are goin' to be the bad actors."
He glanced up and down the street. "Reckon this is the
biggest crowd we ever had in for the show. And they're
not all here yet; there'll be a big bunch over from Green
River on the mornin' train. Does Pike have anythin' to say
to you?"

Grumpy told him no. "He was tryin' to git us where the
hair is short, and he knows we know it. Resa's as friendly
as ever. No reason why she shouldn't be."

After parting with Rainsford, the partners ran into Resa
and Tremaine in front of the Eagle Drug Store. At Stark's
urging, they went in for some ice-cream. Rainbow tried to
keep the conversation off the race but found it impossible.

"The devil will out," Resa said, with a faint smile. "I
know the three of you are thinking of nothing else. Personally, I'll be glad when tomorrow is over. I wish I could
go out and cheer for Johnnie's horse. But I can't; I know
if father loses it's going to be a bitter experience for him."

"If he's entertaining any idea of losing, his talk doesn't
sound like it," Tremaine remarked. "I noticed that Collamore has shortened the odds on Desert Queen. Bushfield's
mare hasn't been given much consideration. Maybe she'll
be the real surprise."

"You really don't believe anything of the sort, Stark,"
Resa told him. "You're convinced Champ will win."

"Maybe I am," he admitted, "but only because I'd like
to see Johnnie get a break. That five-hundred-dollar purse
would mean a lot to him."

Rip and Grumpy sat at the table with their backs to the
street. Resa and Tremaine were facing it. The latter was
speaking, when Resa interrupted him.

"Something has happened," she exclaimed. "I wonder
why everyone is running up the street."

The sheriff had seen the partners enter the drug store.
He appeared in the door suddenly.

"Come on!" he shouted to them. "The stables are afire
at the rodeo grounds!"

"My God!" Grumpy groaned. "They're bone-dry; they'll burn like tinder!"

It was fully a mile from down-town Black Forks to the grounds. Everyone was running that way. A team and wagon came by and the sheriff and the partners and Tremaine piled in.

Suspicion was riding the little man hard.

"This looks like dirty work to me!" he snarled. "I don't believe someone just got careless!"

CHAPTER 18

WHEN THEY REACHED THE GATE they could see that the fire was burning fiercely. Seven or eight stalls had been consumed already.

Howie ran up to them as they leaped down from the wagon.

"Champ's all right!" he yelled. "Snuffy and the Kid led him down by the grandstand! Got him out first thing!"

It was welcome news.

"Where did the fire start?" Rainsford demanded.

"Down at the lower end of the row, Buck!"

Horses were screaming. The handlers and roustabouts were trying to get the frightened animals out of the burning stalls and having a bad time of it. Rainbow ran that way, with the others following. They had gone only a few feet when they heard Pike Kendrick bellowing at the men to save Black Lightning. The roof over the horse's head was ablaze. The sparks from it ignited the straw on the ground.

Sight of the sheriff wrenched a violent outburst from old Pike. "Damn you empty-headed politicians!" he cried. "No water line out here! Not even a fire-barrel!"

A man ran out of Black Lightning's stable, his eyebrows and hair badly singed.

"Try again, Henry!" Kendrick implored wildly. "Put a wet bag over his head! If you don't get him out he'll be a goner in a minute or two!"

"He won't let you git near him, Pike! I had a blanket and he kicked it out of my hands!"

With Champ safe, Johnnie came running back to find that Black Lightning was the only horse that had not been rescued. He found a half-filled water bucket and yelled at Hallett to tear off his shirt.

"Kid, what are you goin' to do?" Grumpy whipped out.

"I'm goin' to git Black Lightnin' out of there! He knows me! I can handle him!"

"Kid, yo're crazy!" the little man protested violently. "You know what Kendrick tried to do to you!"

"It don't matter!" Johnnie answered, dousing Howie's shirt into the water. "I can't see that horse die this way!"

He tore the shirt in two, tied a piece of it over his face, up to his eyes, and darted into the blazing stall.

In the lurid light of the flames he could see the terror-stricken horse, forelegs planted wide, rolling his fear-crazed eyes. He spoke to him, got the halter free. The animal squealed as a burning board from the roof fell across his withers. The Kid knocked it to the ground. His lungs were filling with smoke; he knew he couldn't stay in there long.

"Blackie, it's now or never!" he pleaded. "You got to let me git you out!"

He got the wet shirt over the horse's head, but the animal reared the moment the cloth touched its eyes. The Kid managed to stay with him. Holding the wet rag in place, he grabbed the horse's mane and started to swing up. Before he could make it the rear end of the roof fell in. With hands and shoulders burned, the smoke smothering him, he tried again, and this time he succeeded. When he dug his heels into Black Lightning's belly, the horse plunged out of the flames and smoke with a rush that scattered men right and left. But they cheered as Rainbow lifted the boy down.

"Are you all right, Johnnie?" he asked anxiously. He was proud of the Kid.

"Shore, Rip!" was the doughty answer. "Got burned a bit, but I'm okay."

"Right, nothin'!" Grumpy yelped. "Look at yore hands! How you goin' to ride a race tomorrow?"

"We'll take him into a doctor right away," Rainbow interjected. Pike came up to grumble his thanks. The tall man waved him aside. "This was kindness to a horse, Mr. Kendrick, not to you."

Rip remained for a word with the doctor, after the Kid's hands had been treated and bandaged.

"The burns are not serious, Ripley, but if he rides that race tomorrow it will be on grit alone."

"He's got plenty of that, Doc. He'll be out there, and I'm not going to try to stop him."

Though the stables had been completely destroyed, only one horse had been injured seriously enough to be scratched. The origin of the fire was still in doubt, but Grumpy was forced to admit it had not been aimed at Champ. At Rip's suggestion, he entrusted Andy McBain with the responsibility of getting Mr. Smiley to the show.

"Git him there early, Andy, and buy him whatever he wants. The Kid says he's all right. Wash will have to be satisfied with that. We're goin' out now and we'll be close to him till just about race-time."

They found Champ less affected by the fire than they dared to hope. But as Howie explained, they had led him out and taken him down to the grandstand before the flames had made much headway.

Rip and Grumpy had a talk with Johnnie. The boy's hands were paining him but his spirits had not been dampened.

"You gave me my chance, and I ain't goin' to dog it now. Howie's goin' to take Champ up to the barrier. You didn't fergit Pappy?"

"No, I wouldn't be surprised if Andy and him was up in the grandstand right now," the little one told him. "You ought to eat a sandwich or somethin', Kid."

"I had a couple, Grump. It shore was nice of Mrs. Messenger to send out that basket. You fellas don't want to miss the buckin' contest. You better be gittin' some seats; the crowd's filin' in early."

Rainbow grinned. "I guess that's a hint that we aren't needed here. We'll be pulling hard for you, Johnnie!"

They crossed the track and sat down in the grandstand. The stake race was the third event on the program. Grumpy shook his head when it was announced.

"You need strong hands to ride a race," he muttered. "Grit ain't enough by itself."

"It'll take you a long way," said Rip.

The noise of the crowd and the blaring of the band reached the Kid as Howie and Snuffy lifted him into the saddle to save his hands.

"Nine people out of ten up there are pullin' for you to win, Kid," Snuffy told him. "We'll be waitin' to pick you up when the race is over."

Johnnie gave him a tight-lipped nod and told Howie to get started.

Black Lightning and Desert Queen began to rear as they were led up to the barrier. Seven horses faced the starter. The mare was finally brought into position at the rail, but Kendrick's horse continued to rear. Five times the starter called them back. It made Champ jittery. The Kid groaned as he pulled him down and daggers of pain shot up his arms.

The starter sent them back once more. "Come up slow this time," he warned, "and you keep your horses from breaking, Smiley and Eagen!"

They came back in better line than any previous time. The starter yelled, "Go!" The crowd groaned. It looked for a moment as though Champ had been left flat-footed. But Johnnie got him away. He was last as they passed the grandstand, but going around the first turn he had pulled into fifth place. He had the big horse driving now, and Champ seemed to catch the excitement of the race. Coming into the back stretch, he overhauled Pedroli's Chief.

Desert Queen broke badly and Johnnie shot through along the rail, with only Black Lightning ahead of him.

"Come on, Champ!" he prayed. Biting his lips against the raw torture of his hands, he drove his knees into the buckskin and felt him respond with increased speed. Rounding the far turn, he closed the gap, and as they came into the stretch there was daylight showing between the two horses.

But Black Lightning was not beaten yet. Young Eagen was giving him a good ride. The crowd was on its feet, yelling madly. The wall of noise hit Champ and started to throw him off stride. The Kid clamped down on the rein and straightened him out.

Black Lightning challenged again, but Champ beat him off. Johnnie was beyond anything but keeping himself in the saddle now. He knew Champ was running away with him. He tried to tighten his grip on the rein but his pain-wracked flesh defied his will. His senses were reeling when he flashed under the wire. He knew he had won, but he didn't hear the cheer that went up from the crowd. With his last conscious breath he kicked his feet out of the stirrups and pitched into the dust.

Before the partners could reach him, Howie had rushed out on the track and picked him up.

"Just fainted, I reckon," he said to Rip. "His hands must been painin' him somethin' awful!"

It proved to be a correct diagnosis. When Johnnie opened his eyes his head was pillowed in Resa Kendrick's lap. He gazed at her and the partners a long time before he said, "I won, Rip. I told you Champ wouldn't let us down." He smiled wanly. "Will you collect my prize money for me?"

"You'll have to do that yourself, Johnnie. Tomorrow will be time enough."

Dan and Buck pushed through the circle. They had Doc Treadway with them. "He's got a bad fall," the latter told the partners. "The thing to do is to take him to the hospital. If he isn't hurt, so much the better; he can use a little rest and quiet. We can borrow a rig from somebody."

"I've got one if you'll use it," Pike Kendrick offered.

"I'll go with you and hold him," Resa offered. "You can drive, Mr. Messenger."

Rainbow lifted the boy and carried him to the rig. "We'll follow you, Dan," he said as they were pulling away.

With Rainsford, the partners hurried to the hospital. They found Messenger in the reception room.

"Doc says there's no broken bones," he was able to tell them. "Resa and the nurse are cleaning him up and putting him to bed. It may be a few minutes before we can go in."

They had sat there some time when Buck said, in his drawling tone, "I stopped at Arrowhead one night when I was out lookin' for the Kid. Kendrick told me somethin' that's stuck in my mind. He said it was strange how Johnnie had worked for him, just a kind of ranch roustabout, earnin' a few dollars a month, and now everythin' was revolvin' around him. It seems to be that way with us. If we haven't taken him under our wings already, we better do it—and I don't mean for a week or a few months."

"We'll have to do something for him," Dan agreed. "We can afford to make things easier for him. The purse will give Johnnie a little nest egg to start with."

"Don't count on the purse, Dan," Rainbow spoke up. "There may not be much of it left when the doctors get through with it. He wanted the money so he could do something for his father. No matter what we think about it, we can't deny him that, and I'm not convinced that any doctor in Black Forks is competent to say it will be money wasted. The first thing for us to do is to see him through it. But Grump and I will go all the way with you. Johnnie's only a boy, but he gave this community a lesson in unselfishness last night that'll be remembered long after the race is forgotten."

Resa appeared in the doorway.

"Wal, can we go in?" Grumpy asked.

"He's sound asleep," she said, her eyes a little misty. "He had me put his watch under his pillow. He told me you had brought it to him from Denver, Rainbow. It was a wonderful investment. He held it up for me to see, and he said, 'Resa, you know if any watch you bought in Black Fork's got a fall like that, it woulda busted wide open, but Rip's watch never missed a tick'."

The others laughed, but Grumpy scowled self-accusingly. "By grab, that watch chain!" he muttered. "I plumb forgot all about it!"

Bliss Lomax was a pseudonym for **Harry Sinclair Drago,** born in 1888 in Toledo, Ohio. Drago quit Toledo University to become a reporter for the Toledo *Bee*. He later turned to writing fiction with *Suzanna: A Romance Of Early California*, published by Macauley in 1922. In 1927 he was in Hollywood, writing screenplays for Tom Mix and Buck Jones. In 1932 he went East, settling in White Plains, New York, where he concentrated on writing Western fiction for the magazine market, above all for Street & Smith's *Western Story Magazine*, to which he had contributed fiction as early as 1922. Many of his novels, written under the pseudonyms Bliss Lomax and Will Ermine, were serialised prior to book publication in magazines. Some of the best of these were also made into films. The Bliss Lomax titles *Colt Comrades* (Doubleday, Doran, 1939) and *The Leather Burners* (Doubleday, Doran, 1940) were filmed as superior entries in the Hopalong Cassidy series with William Boyd, *Colt Comrades* (United Artists, 1943) and *Leather Burners* (United Artists, 1943). At his best Drago wrote Western stories that are tightly plotted with engaging characters, and often it is suspense that comprises their pulse and dramatic pacing.